THE WAR WITHIN OUR PUBLIC SCHOOLS

Joseph A. Colosimo

iUniverse, Inc.
New York   Bloomington

The War Within Our Public Schools

iUniverse books may be ordered through booksellers or by contacting:

iUniverse
1663 Liberty Drive
Bloomington, IN 47403
www.iuniverse.com
1-800-Authors (1-800-288-4677)

Because of the dynamic nature of the Internet, any Web addresses or
links contained in this book may have changed since publication and
may no longer be valid. The views expressed in this work are solely those
of the author and do not necessarily reflect the views of the publisher, and
the publisher hereby disclaims any responsibility for them.

ISBN: 978-1-4401-5747-9 (sc)
ISBN: 978-1-4401-5746-2 (ebk)

Printed in the United States of America

iUniverse rev. date: 07/14/2009

To Lisa for believing in me

Thank you to my family for all their support; my mentors Hector La Marque and Curt Joiner for constantly pushing me to get better; my friends past and present who kept telling me to get this done; all the warriors at PFS for inspiring me; Dr. David Esselstrom; Joe Thomas at Van Kampen; and to my Lord Jesus Christ. In memory of my dad, Archie Colosimo and Brian Holm.

Cover Illustration by Lisa Colosimo

CHAPTER 1

Early in the morning a group of students gathered around the flag pole in front of their school and began to pray. It was the annual *See You at the Pole* morning of prayer. The local churches encouraged the Christian children to pray for their school, the staff, the students, and their Nation. This was voluntary, and year after year a large group of students, parents, and occasional school staff showed up and prayed in front of their schools.

Ms. Wallace had just pulled up in the parking lot when she saw the crowd of students. She took out her cell phone and made a call.

"Good morning, Ev. I just pulled up to the school. It must be that pray-around-the-pole day again. All the little church kids are in a big circle around the flag. Isn't there something we can do about this?"

"Unfortunately, it's legal," Ev answered back, "but we're working on it."

"These people have got to be stopped!"

"They'll get theirs during Tolerance Week. The District has some good gay speakers lined up for them."

"That will be fun to watch. I'll talk to you later."

Inside the school, the assistant principal was dealing with the situation as well.

"I want this stopped!" the short, balding man commanded. "There is a separation of Church and State, and my child's rights are being violated by that crowd of students."

"Mr. Green, how are her rights being violated by that crowd of students?" the assistant principal asked.

"They are praying in public! *That* is not allowed!" he said with his finger pointed at the administrator.

"Mr. Green, I'm not trying to be rude, but you may want to check your Constitution," she suggested. "There is a Right of Assembly, and the school is not sponsoring this. Those students gathered under their own free will."

"Aren't their teachers out there too?"

"Yes, but they also have the same right. They did not organize this. Most of the local churches encouraged the children that attend them to pray for their schools. They're not violating any laws."

"I'm contacting my lawyer and congressman. This is going to stop! It's not fair to my daughter."

"By all means, you can do that, Mr. Green. Can I ask you a question, though?"

"What?"

"Would you rather see students doing graffiti and vandalizing their school or praying for it?"

The man angrily turned and left the office.

~

It was fourth period, and that meant health education class. It always seemed like more than "health" education though to Lisa Kaye. It was more like Ms. Wallace's opinion of health. This class always made Lisa feel uncomfortable, but today it was even more uncomfortable. Today was day one of sex education, though it seemed more like just sex.

"Today we're going to be discussing practicing safe sex," Ms. Wallace started. Laughter and cheers began to break out. "I will not tolerate immaturity while teaching this subject, so settle down now!" Ms. Wallace was in her mid-fifties. Her brown hair was graying and her body was thinning. It was a rare event when the students saw her smile. Almost immediately a hand went up. "Yes, Tammy. You have a question already?"

"Don't you mean *safer* sex?" the fourteen-year-old, red-headed girl asked.

"The State of California has approved this curriculum to make sure that when you teenagers decide to go have sex, you'll be protected," Ms. Wallace replied with obvious annoyance.

"But my mom says there's no such thing as *safe* sex,"

Tammy shot back, "There's only *safer* sex. And what if I choose not to have sex until I'm married?"

The teacher was becoming very irritated now. "Miss Ramirez, your mother is mistaken. It's a proven *fact* that at some point in time, teenagers *will* have sex. They're no different from animals. It's human instinct. I'm here to make sure you protect yourselves properly when that time comes."

"You're saying that I don't have the ability to choose not to?" Tammy persisted.

"I'm not going to have this discussion anymore, Miss Ramirez!" Ms. Wallace was turning red now, "The facts are the facts."

"Whose facts?" Tammy did not let up.

"Leave my room and go to the office now, Miss Ramirez!" She yelled while pointing at the door.

"She's just asking a question," Brian Holm said in Tammy's defense, "And I'd like to know whose facts too."

"Great! You can discuss it with Tammy on the way to the office!"

She went over to a switch on the wall and flicked it up. In a few seconds a voice from a loud speaker called out: "Yes, Ms. Wallace?"

"I'm sending two defiant students to Mrs. Faretti's office. I'm through with them disrupting my class."

"We'll be expecting them," the voice said back.

Ms. Wallace looked at the two students. "Out! Now!" And Tammy and Brian followed the orders.

Lisa Kaye sat quietly watching the whole scene. She agreed with Tammy, but she did not want to end up in her current situation. *I hate this class,* she thought to herself.

~

After class, Lisa saw her best friend, Autumn, in the hall. "Hey, what's happening?" Autumn asked.

"I hate that class!" Lisa responded, "And you better watch out: 'Wallace the Witch' is on her broom today."

"Oh, great! Just what I needed right now." Autumn had the health class next. "Is she on the broom or on the rag?" It was a weak attempt at humor.

Lisa ignored the comment, "She was having us put condoms on bananas."

"Oh, it's sex time," Autumn said with a smile. "This ought to be good. So what's wrong with that? Haven't you seen a condom before?"

"No, and I didn't need to either. That lady thinks we're all going to go out and have sex as soon as possible. She thinks we're no better than animals. Not a chance!"

"Hey, you never know," Autumn replied. "Some stud, football guy in high school next year might ask you to the Prom, and who knows where you might end up."

Lisa was in no mood for this, "Look, you may be my best friend, but in some areas we're not alike. I'm a Christian, and I believe what the Bible says. And you know where I stand on this, so cut it out. I come from a very different family than yours."

Lisa had known Autumn for six years now. Autumn's mom frequently bragged about being "A Child of the '70s." Mr. and Mrs. Woods were nice people, though Lisa rarely ever saw them at the same time. Both had full-time jobs and were not home much, especially Mr. Woods. Autumn and her older sister, Summer, frequently had free reign of the house. There were always high school guys at the house when Lisa would visit with Autumn. It made Lisa feel uneasy sometimes. Autumn rolled her eyes up when she told Lisa that her mom gave them '70s names. Autumn was a tall blonde with blue eyes. She was fourteen, but she looked older, and that sat well with her.

Lisa's parents, on the other hand, were as conservative as they come. Lisa grew up going to church, and she always loved it. Her parents had flirted with the idea of home schooling on more than one occasion, but they felt that their daughter should see what the world is like. After all, she would find out sooner or later. Lisa was about five-foot one with long dark hair and brilliant green eyes. Unlike her friend, she looked younger than her age. Her dad ran a financial services business, and her mom stayed home. Her parents were very active in their church. Lisa had an older brother named Chris, whom she enjoyed picking on and bugging, like little sisters are supposed to do. Her parents loved to read to her and teach her through the Bible, and Lisa grew up to know it as the Truth. Ever since Autumn's family moved into her area six years ago, Lisa had been trying with no success to get Autumn to go to church with her. Autumn would say it was not for her. Lisa's mom would tell her to always keep Autumn and her family in prayer. Even though the two girls came from such different backgrounds, they were still best of friends.

"I'm sorry," Autumn backed off, "I didn't realize you were that worked up."

"I am, and I don't know how much longer I can stay in this school."

"Hey, you're not the only Christian here," Autumn observed. "Don't Brian and Tammy go to your church?"

"Yeah, they do," Lisa replied, "and who do you think she's always singling out? And she told the lady at the office that they were being defiant. Why? Because they didn't buy in to her safe sex crap—and that's what it is— crap! People get pregnant and get diseases no matter how safe they're trying to be."

"Well, the good news is, it's only one unit," Autumn tried to encourage her.

"But it's more than that. We have to hear her political views too. And you know that if you don't agree with her, your grade gets killed."

"Has that happened to you?"

Lisa hesitated, "No, but only because I pretend to agree with her."

"Well, enough of this stuff," Autumn decided to change the subject. "I'm meeting with Jorge tonight."

"Tonight?" Lisa said surprised. "Tonight's Monday. Do your parents know?"

Autumn made a "raspberry-sounding" noise, "Yeah, right! Besides, neither one of them will be home anyway."

"Why not?" Lisa asked. "It doesn't seem like they're ever home."

"They hardly are," Autumn said with a smile, "that's what's so great about it. We get the whole house to ourselves. They really don't get along either"

"Where's Summer going to be?"

"Who knows . . . out partying with her friends, most likely." Autumn said nonchalantly.

Lisa was concerned now, "Hey, don't do this. Jorge is much older than you. You don't want to be alone with him."

"I like that he's much older than me. Do you think I want to go out with the little boys here?" Autumn said sarcastically. "Besides, he's such a stud. How many junior high girls do you know that get to go out with a junior in high school?"

"That's my point," Lisa said, "Not many at all. They shouldn't be."

"I think you're going a little too virgin on me, Lisa."

"Have you . . . ever . . . you know?" Lisa attempted to ask.

"Not all the way yet, no," Autumn replied.

"Autumn, I really care about you. You're like a sister to me. I don't want anything to happen to you. The Bible says it's for marriage only."

"Lisa, the Bible was written a long time ago. Times have changed. Besides, I'll be careful. I won't let things go farther than they should—if I even allow them to go anywhere at all."

"All I know is that it's supposed to be for a husband and a wife."

"Well, like I said, times have changed. Maybe you should take in a little more carefully what Ms. Wallace is teaching us." Autumn said it from her heart, but it did not sit well with Lisa.

"I think Ms. Wallace needs to read the Bible." She looked her friend in the eyes and almost pleaded, "Autumn, please don't be alone with Jorge tonight."

"I'll be okay. I trust him."

CHAPTER 2

Brian Holm's mother got the phone call from Mrs. Faretti. "Hello, Mrs. Holm. This is Mrs. Faretti at George Washington Junior High." It seemed every city had at least one school named after the first president.

"Hello, Mrs. Faretti," Mrs. Holm replied, "Is everything all right with Brian?"

"Well," Kim was a little hesitant, "Brian was kicked out of his class today for defiance."

Mrs. Holm was taken by surprise. "Wow, Mrs. Faretti! I have to admit that I'm surprised to hear that. Brian is certainly not a perfect kid, but I haven't known him to be defiant either. Which class was he defiant in, Mrs. Faretti?"

"His health class," the second-year assistant principal responded.

"Mrs. Faretti, I want you to know that I'm not one of those my-little-angel-would-never-do-that parents,"

Linda Holm began. "My son has made numerous comments about his health teacher—all negative. He can't stand Ms. Wallace. When we were at the school's Back to School Night. She came across professionally, but not friendly. I did not get a good vibe from the woman, but it was a first encounter. Brian has told me many times that he feels like Ms. Wallace hates the boys. He told me that most of the boys in the room just keep quiet. He has also told me about the numerous political comments she makes, which makes me wonder what that has to do with health. What's Brian's story about what happened, Mrs. Faretti?"

"Brian said that he had just asked Ms. Wallace a question after another student had spoken—something about teenagers having sex."

"Teenagers having sex? What's going on in that classroom, Mrs. Faretti?" Linda asked with elevated curiosity.

"It's their sexual education unit, Mrs. Holm, and it doesn't surprise me if some of the kids get squirrelly," Kim responded.

Now Linda was angry, "Why wasn't I, the parent, notified about this?"

"I'm not sure I understand, Mrs. Holm." Kim was being careful now, but at the same time she wanted to be straight with the woman. "The school is not required to notify the parents about this. Ms. Wallace is just teaching the California, State-approved curriculum."

"Did it ever occur to the school and the State that I don't want my son learning about this from them?" Linda almost yelled.

"It's not an optional course, Mrs. Holm," Kim replied. "Health is a required class, and sex ed. is part of it."

"I don't have a choice?" It was not really a question. There was silence for a brief moment. "Okay, something tells me that this is another discussion for a later time, but a very soon time." She got back to Brian. "Mrs. Faretti, has Brian been sent up to your office for defiance before?"

Kim quickly brought Brian's discipline record up on her computer, but in actuality, she knew that she did not need to. Assistant principals usually know when they have seen a student in their office for discipline. They have their "regular attenders" and their "once-in-awhiles." Brian was not either of them. He had no discipline record. In fact, just the opposite, he had been named Student of the Month and was on the Honor Roll all last year as a seventh grader and the first quarter of this year. Kim knew that Mrs. Holm had her—Brian was one of the best students in the school. "No, Mrs. Holm; he hasn't."

"Were any other students sent up to you from this class?" Linda probed.

Kim hated this now, "I'm not allowed to discuss other students with you, Mrs. Holm. I'm sorry." *I can't tell you that Tammy was sent too, and that she is also an Honor Roll student, but I'm sure your son will tell you, and soon I'll have her mom to deal with too,* she thought to herself.

"Is Brian there with you right now, Mrs. Faretti?"

"He's just outside the door. Would you like to speak with him?" she asked politely.

"Yes, I would, thank you."

Kim asked Brian to come in. She pushed a button on the phone. "Mrs. Holm, Brian is here, and I put you on speaker."

"Brian, what happened?" his mother enquired. Brian proceeded to tell his mother what happened in the classroom. "So you wanted to know her sources as well?"

"Mom, I didn't like the way she was treating Tammy, but I also felt that if she was going to say that it was a *fact*, I wanted to know. You and Dad have told us that we have a choice."

"Brian, I want you to go back out." His mom told him. Brian left the room, and Kim took the phone off speaker. "Mrs. Faretti." Linda began, "I'm not the type of parent that believes my son can do no wrong, and I'm not about to defend him in front of another adult, because I know what that can create. He's a teenage boy, and he can be a handful at home . . ."

Here comes the "but," Kim thought to herself.

". . . but, right now, I'm struggling not to believe every word he's just said. I don't know Ms. Wallace, but I will say that at Back to School Night, she did rub me the wrong way—a militant-type . . ."

Wow, you're good with first impressions, lady, Kim thought again, *if you only knew what a pain in the butt she really is!*

". . . Mrs. Faretti, what is your gut feeling about this?

Kim could not say what she was feeling. "Mrs. Holm, I'd like to get back to you a little later. I think for right now, I'm going to let Brian do his work up here at the office until the bell rings. Lunch is next, and I'm going to try and track down Ms. Wallace and get more information."

"That sounds good," Linda said. "I'll wait to hear from you later. Thank you."

Kim hung up the phone angry. Ms. Wallace caused her more grief than any other teacher at the school. She was always ticking off somebody. If it was not a student, it was a parent; if it was not a parent, it was another teacher. She was the epitome of misery breeds company.

Kim was only in her early thirties. She had taught for five years and decided to try her hand at administration. Her days were getting longer at work all the time, and Kim often felt fatigued and nauseous when she finally got home to her family. What once was an exciting opportunity to move up in the education system was quickly breaking her down.

CHAPTER 3

James Kaye was doing what he loved to do, helping people and making a difference. It sounded corny, but that is what he loved to do. The bonus was that he made great money doing it. He had been in the financial field for seven years now. But seven years ago, he knew nothing about it. In fact, when he was first approached about coming on board with his company, he made it clear to the young man trying to recruit him that if he had to do math, someone was going to lose money. But the young man insisted that all he had to do was get the important information from the client, put it into the computer, and the computer program would do the rest. In reality there was a learning curve, but James was willing to learn. He was in his late thirties when he was approached and figured that it was now or never if he was going to make a move. He had been a junior high English teacher for ten years and a school assistant principal for four years after that. The public school system had completely fried him and taken its toll on his health. He knew he had to do something different. But what? All he was qualified for was education. He was given the same message that everyone else got—go to school, graduate, go to college, get a degree, and get a "safe, secure job with benefits."

James did all that and more. He got two degrees and a graduate after that. So why did he have nowhere to go now that he was completely dissatisfied with his job? He quickly figured out that his degrees did not open all the doors like the scholars told him. It was just the opposite; they narrowed them down. He was only qualified for one thing—education. He actually loved educating people. It was the system he was in that he hated. When the young man approached him about a business opportunity that he could change other people's lives with and get financially free at the same time, the timing was perfect for James.

The company itself was huge, and James was not a "corporate America" kind of guy. In fact, corporate America was a major turn off for him. But there was a part of this company that allowed ambitious, self-motivated, people to have the opportunity to have their own business and, at the same time, help people with financial education. James had no experience with finances, but he had many good people in the company willing to help him learn. It was not long before James was teaching others how to do it and running his own business. He loved it. He was educating people, making a difference, changing his own family's life, and getting wealthy at the same time with no boss or screwed-up system. In that seven year stretch, he had read more books than he did in his eleven years of college. He quickly figured out that self-education was significantly greater than formal, classroom education—a lesson that he had already passed on to his wife Bethany and was in the process of passing on to his son Chris and daughter Lisa.

After reading books like *Rich Dad, Poor Dad, 177 Mental Toughness Secrets of the World Class, The 21 Irrefutable Laws of Leadership, The Purpose Driven Life,* and many others that had impacted his life and helped him self-develop, he quickly figured out that formal education was good, but it would never take someone to greatness. It was too bad the public school system would never figure that out. Bethany and he had debated taking their children out of the system and either home schooling or enrolling them into a private, Christian school. But Chris and Lisa had many good friends at their schools, and they liked most of their teachers, so for now, they would stay.

He was driving in his SUV when his cell phone rang. The caller I.D. said Bethany. "Hi, Baby," he said to Bethany.

"What time should I have dinner ready for you?" she enquired.

"I'm seeing a family at 6:00 and another at 8:00. Can

we have an early dinner at 5:00?" Most of the families James met with were only able to get together in the evening, so it was common for his family to have early dinners. James did not mind. He got to have breakfast, lunch, and dinner with his family most days. The majority of the families he served rarely got to be together with their families for more than two hours. They believed in the system—have a "safe, secure job." That always made James laugh, *J*O*B—Just Over Broke!* And that is how many of his clients were. It was sad. They had no family time, not enough money, more than enough debt, and no life.

"Five works for me," Bethany said. "Hey, just an FYI, your daughter came home pretty upset from school today."

"Oh, what's up?" James asked.

"She seems to think that one of her teachers was out of line with a couple of her friends. If it happened like she says, the teacher pulled rank when the kids wouldn't just buy-in to every word she said. So much for allowing for learning and self-discovery."

"Which teacher was it?" he asked.

"The health teacher, Ms. Wallace. Do you remember her from the Back to School Night?"

"Was she the one I wanted to smack?"

Bethany could not help to laugh. James had a way with sarcasm. "Yep, that's the one."

"Ask Lisa if she wants me to go smack her," James said with a smile.

"I think I'll pass on that one," Bethany said, "but I think this is worth a discussion tonight."

"Looking forward to it. I'll see you at 5:00. I love you, Baby."

"Love you too," and they hung up.

James was extremely in love with his wife. They had been together for thirteen years and married for twelve. It was strange how they met. James had just finished his Masters degree that year. He was living in his own bachelor's pad, a two bedroom condo with one bath. It had been three years since his last relationship, which did not end well. He decided to stay focused on completing his Masters after that. But once he was done, he told God that he now had time for a relationship, and if God was ready, so was he.

All of James' closest friends had already married, and one had already divorced. He saw that, did not like it, and reasoned that he would rather stay single the rest of his life than marry the wrong person. Besides, he was not completely alone. He had a parrot to keep him company, and a cable television that pumped Lakers' basketball to him once in awhile. He was only five-foot eight, but he was in good shape.

James was asked by his church that summer to direct a singles' camp up in Sequoia National Forest. Two weeks after that, he would go back up and co-direct a junior high camp. He was twenty-eight at the time with a quickly receding hair line and figured that if he could not meet a girl at singles camp, he had better join the CIA. After the first week, the singles' camp, it was looking like the CIA was going to have a new recruit. Two weeks later at that same camp, he met a young lady on staff, who was actually there two weeks prior, but he never saw her. James figured it was because she was so young looking. Bethany was very petite with long, dark brown hair. But the most striking feature about her was her cat-like, light-green eyes. When James first laid eyes on her, he just thought she was a cute little girl (she only looked sixteen). When he found out that she was twenty-two, he paid closer attention.

Bethany was shy at first, but she quickly opened up to the man that would be her fiancé four months after that week. A year later, they were married. Four years after that, they had Chris. James knew that if he did not leave the education field, he would have never have had a child. He also knew that that would not have been fair to Bethany, who strongly desired to have one. James had hoped for a boy. He knew that boys were tougher than girls when they were young, but he also knew from his previous experience as a teacher and assistant principal that teen-age girls could be a father's nightmare. The good news was that God had blessed him with a beautiful and well-behaved daughter as a second child. She ended up with her mother's green eyes as opposed to his brown. Lisa was strongly involved in her church youth group, and it was rare when she missed a Sunday school class or a Wednesday night gathering. Someday—in about twenty-five years, if James had his way—there was going to be a very lucky guy out there who would marry his daughter.

He could not help but wonder what Bethany's concern was regarding Lisa's health teacher. In his time of being in the California public school system, he had learned that there were many people at all levels that had their own political agendas. They also had no problem whatsoever about shoving them down the children's throats. It was unethical and even could be considered grounds for termination. Of course, that would never happen. The teachers were heavily protected by the Teacher's Union, which, in turn, was heavily backed by left-wing politicians. It amazed him how so many politicians thought that they could raise another person's child better than their parents. In recent years, the liberal California legislatures had very quietly passed many laws that were taking more and more power away from parents. The most recent one allowed minor girls to be able to receive an abortion without her parent's consent and knowledge. The very thought of that raised the hairs on the back of James' neck. When the media had announced—down-right celebrated---the law being passed, James and Bethany were furious. "I've got to be honest with you, Honey," James had told Bethany, "if anyone ever touched my little girl that way without my knowledge, they'd be dead, and you'd never get to see me again." Bethany had told him not to worry;

Lisa had her act together. James believed that too, but his experience as an assistant principal had shown him that even the best little girls could get themselves in some pretty awful situations. The good news was that he and Bethany had extremely good open communication with Lisa. Just the same, this all-out attack on families and children by these '60s, "if-it-feels-good-do-it" freaks infuriated James. *God will judge them,* he thought, *In the meantime, keep praying.*

CHAPTER 4

"You asked to see me, Kim?" Jo Ann Wallace came to Kim's door. "Oh, did you get those two brats I sent to you?"

"That's why I sent for you," Kim replied, "Will you please shut the door and sit down."

Ms. Wallace complied. "Is something wrong?"

"I'd like to know what exactly happened today in your fourth period class. I want to know why two students that have never been sent to my office before, including last year, were suddenly class suspended today." Kim's tone was calm but direct.

Ms. Wallace became defensive though. "Are you accusing me of something, Kim?" She did not bother to wait for an answer. "Because I don't need to remind you that I have been teaching for over twenty years, and I think I know when a student—or students—are disrupting a class."

"I said I'd like to know what happened." Her voice remained level.

Ms. Wallace gave her version of what took place in her classroom. She spoke of the State-approved curriculum and the "factual" information. "It's not my fault that the girl's misinformed mother gave her bad information, and that her little friend had to try and play the knight in shiny armor."

"Jo Ann," Kim began, "These parents want explanations as to why their children got thrown out of a class. In my conversations with both parents, they both acknowledged that they didn't raise little angels; but at the same time, neither of them has had an incident like this ever come up. Both students' discipline records show no previous behavior like this."

"So what's your point?" Ms. Wallace interrupted boldly.

That did not sit well with Kim. She suddenly straightened up in her chair, and the expression on her face got strong. "My *point*, Ms. Wallace, is that from what I'm hearing from you and the students is that there were differing views in your room, and when yours got challenged, you pulled rank."

"I don't give views, Kim!" Ms. Wallace was turning red. "I gave them the facts of the State-approved curriculum."

"Really?" Kim was quick to counter. "I had no idea that everything in the State-approved curriculum was a *proven* fact. Let me ask you this: Do you honestly believe that every teen-age kid in the world, due to their complete incapability of thinking for themselves and controlling their animal-like sexual urges, will just at some point in time strip off their clothes and go have sex?"

Ms. Wallace was glaring. Kim could see she was burning up, and she decided to cool the situation off. "Jo Ann, I know that you're a strong advocate for women's rights," she was careful about how she worded things. "This young lady, she was telling you that she is a free-thinking female. She was trying to say that, in spite of what the entire State-approved curriculum in the world might think, she can think for herself. You should applaud her for her boldness and self-confidence—especially at such a young age."

Ms. Wallace loosened up. Kim could see Ms. Wallace's facial expression which showed that she liked what she heard. "I guess I didn't look at it that way. She's exercising her right to choose. She certainly is a sharp young woman." Her expression got angry again, "But what about the boy? He has no excuse."

"What is our goal as educators?" It was a rhetorical question. "Is it to instill our personal beliefs upon the students, or is it to help them think and discover for themselves? The fact is that Brian's question, as much as it may have annoyed you, was fair and legitimate. Maybe he could have asked with a better tone, I agree. But he was doing the exact same thing as Tammy—he was thinking for himself. Jo Ann, there's a big difference between being defiant and questioning the quote unquote facts."

"It disrupted the whole class," she said in response.

"Jo Ann," Kim stopped for a breath, "I'm going to shoot straight with you. What it did was send a message to every other student in the class that if they disagree with you—"

"It's in the book!" She abruptly cut in.

"It doesn't matter, Jo Ann." Kim came right back. "The message is still that if they disagree with you—or the book—they lose. Last I checked, we still live in America. I'm sure you and I have some different beliefs too," *Significant ones*, she thought to herself, "But that doesn't make me your enemy. On the other hand, if you make me feel that way for my beliefs, the chances of me talking with you again become more infrequent. Do you see what I mean?"

"I still have to show the other students who's in charge of the classroom. I can't just allow these misfits to try and take over."

"But that's the part you can control. You can set the rules and guidelines for class discussion. If they're not going to discuss something within the guidelines, then it turns to discipline." Again, Kim took a breath. "Jo Ann, you teach health ed. There are going to be some major controversial topics. There should be healthy discussion on both sides of the topics. And one more thing: Take a look at this." Kim turned her computer screen so Ms.

Wallace could see it. At the top of the screen it said DISCIPLINE. It then showed the student's name, and the record of discipline history. The name was Brian Holm. "Look at this misfit's discipline record." There was nothing there. Kim then hit another key. The screen changed to ACADEMIC RECORD. Brian's grades were displayed from last year. His Grade Point Average came to 3.88. "Jo Ann, this is a really good kid. It would be my dream as an assistant principal to have every boy in the school with his academic and discipline records. I wouldn't have to be here for ten hours a day."

"All right," Ms. Wallace said with a, sort of, surrender in her voice. "I get the picture. I don't want them to look at me as some dictator teacher. Is that it?"

"As far as I'm concerned, yes. I'll leave it up to you on how you want to handle this with the students. Thanks for your time."

Ms. Wallace left the room. Kim was mentally exhausted. *Please retire soon!* She said to herself.

~

The dinner table conversation was typically pleasant in the Kaye house, but tonight was a bit different. Lisa was speaking to her parents about the events in Ms. Wallace's class. "Mom, the only ones she really gets on are the Christians. She is constantly saying stuff that goes against everything you've taught me and what I've learned from Pastor Mike at church." Pastor Mike Davies was the church youth pastor. He was well-respected by the parents and the children.

"Lisa," her mother began, "do you think that you might be taking this too hard? I mean, isn't she just doing her job?"

"Do you believe that?" James cut in.

Bethany shot a look of annoyance towards her husband.

"I don't," Chris threw in his two cents. "I had her too. She was the same way when I was there."

"Why didn't you ever say anything to Mom and Dad about it?" Lisa asked.

"I don't know. I guess it didn't bug me enough. I knew enough to just keep my mouth shut when I was in her class."

"Wow! What a great learning environment!" James said sarcastically. "I used to have a name for teachers like that when I was an AP: EGR, Extra Grace Required."

"Well, I'm tired of her bagging on my Christian friends," Lisa said.

"Try to stay calm when you're in her class, honey, and pray for her," Bethany suggested.

"You mean to get run over by a bus?" Chris asked with a smile. James could not help to smirk.

"You guys are no help," Bethany said.

CHAPTER 5

It was 6:30 P.M. when Autumn Woods' door bell rang. She was the only one home to answer it. Her mother had called her an hour earlier to say she would be very late, there was food in the fridge, and lock the door before she goes to bed. Her father was out of town on a business trip. Autumn had called Jorge and told him that they had the house to themselves.

Autumn opened the door, and Jorge smiled. He was pleased at what he saw. Autumn had put on her shortest shorts she had and a loosely-fit top with only a few buttons fastened. Jorge had a bag in his hand. He told Autumn that he had managed to "score some drinks." The bag contained a bottle of rum and a couple cans of Coke. Autumn made some pop corn and rented a DVD for them to watch. After a couple drinks, the movie quickly got boring.

~

Dena Woods finally got home from work at 11:48 P.M. She was told that the corporate world would be a paradise; that she would have fulfillment and a sense of importance. She took an executive assistant job at her company over five years ago. Her family needed the extra money. She would voluntarily work over time with no extra compensation. Her superiors were so impressed with her work ethic and dedication that they promoted her up the company ladder. But each promotion meant more hours as well as some travel. Being Summer and Autumn's mother began to take a back seat. Her Husband, Curt, was already doing the corporate life. He was always traveling. Dena strongly suspected him of having an affair with his secretary. Their marriage was coming apart quickly. The last thing she wanted to have happen in her late thirties was a divorce and starting over again. She had watched some of her friends that had gone through it, and they were all miserable.

All she wanted to do was go to bed. She walked in the dark house and saw her younger daughter sleeping on the couch. *Poor girl,* she thought to herself, *she must have tried to wait up for me.* Dena did not have the heart to wake her. Instead, she went into her bedroom, took off her work clothes, and was quickly asleep.

CHAPTER 6

Lisa and Autumn had a couple of classes together in their school schedules, P.E. and history. Lisa liked her P.E. teacher, Mr. Michaels. He always tried hard to praise the students and kept an optimistic attitude. Her history teacher, Mr. Norburg was okay, but Lisa felt like sometimes he would try to put too many different spins on history. After all, history is what it is . . . history.

As Lisa and Autumn were sitting in their history class, Lisa could not help but notice how lethargic Autumn was this morning. "You look like you didn't sleep," Lisa said.

"No, I did," replied Autumn, "It was just a long night. Jorge stayed longer than I expected. I feel bad because I must have fallen asleep on the guy."

"What do you mean? Don't you know?" Lisa questioned her.

"Well, we were watching the movie—for the most

part—and he brought some drinks, and all I know is that I woke up on the couch this morning."

"What kind of drinks?" Lisa persisted.

"You know what kind." The bell to begin class rang at that moment. "We'll talk later."

Mr. Norburg stood at the front of the room. He was about 5'9" with Coke-bottle-thick glasses. His hair was not combed, and his students were used to seeing him look that way. He wore a striped, short-sleeve shirt and gray slacks. His shoes had seen better days. In the words of his students, he was a geek. But in spite of all that, most of his students thought he was nice.

"Class," he began, "today I'm going to give you an assignment that will be due a week from today. Imagine you could go back in time and interview a historical figure—George Washington, Plato, Shakespeare, Martin Luther King, and so on. If you got to interview them, what would you find out? I want you to research a famous person of history and write a biography about that person. Now, when I say history, I mean that I would like you to go back at least twenty years." Mr. Norburg went on to give the requirements of the essay that was due.

Lisa liked the idea of this assignment. Her mental wheels were already spinning. She did not think twice about the person she was going to research. Some of the other students were moaning a little about it though.

After class Lisa and Autumn walked out together. "Who are you going to research," Lisa asked Autumn.

"I don't know yet. This seems like it's going to be a lot of work though. It's going to take away from phone and guy time," Autumn said.

"Speaking of *guy time*," Lisa began, "what happened last night?"

"Everything was cool. We watched a movie, had a couple rum and Cokes, kissed a bit, and then I fell asleep. I felt bad."

"And that was it?" Lisa persisted.

"That was it," Autumn said.

"I really worry about you, girl."

"Don't. I'm fine."

Lisa paused for a minute. "Autumn, we're friends, right?" she asked.

Autumn gave her a perplexed look. "Of course we are. You're my best friend. You don't think I have these conversations with anyone else, do you?"

"I hope not," Lisa replied. "If word got around here, your rep would be toast. But here's the thing, you're my best friend too. I care about you. When I hear you telling me about your wild nights, it really concerns me. I pray for you all the time."

"You pray for me?" Autumn said with a bit of sarcasm. "I'm not *that* bad."

"You don't have to be bad to have someone pray for you. I just pray that God will keep my best friend safe."

Autumn went quiet, and for a brief moment, Lisa saw her get teary-eyed. But she quickly toughened up.

Two boys were walking by as the girls were speaking. "Hi, Lisa," Brian Holm said. His friend Ken Schilling pushed him slightly, and he brushed up against Lisa. She waved and smiled back.

~

"You really like her, don't you?" Ken asked Brian.

"I think she's really cute and nice, and her eyes are beautiful," Brian said.

"She's one of those *good girls,* dude. You'll never get anywhere with her," Ken antagonized his friend a bit.

"Dude, shut up!" Brian was angry. "That really ticks me off! I think she's nice and pretty. I like it that she's different from the other girls here. Don't talk that way about her"

"Sorry, man," Ken replied. "I didn't mean to get to you. She is nice and pretty."

"Ken, if I wanted to have sex, I could get with Jasmine Stone."

"I won't argue that one," Ken said. "Did you see what she's wearing today?"

"Yes, that's my point." Brian replied. "Did you see all the guys with their tongues hanging out?"

"Mine included," Ken had to add.

"I don't want a girl who attracts the attention of *every* guy around. That girl knows every guy. My dad told me, when a girl knows too many guys, you're just another one."

"Do you think she's as loose as everyone says?" Ken asked.

"In all honesty," Brian began, "yes I do. She has no problem dressing like she's been with every guy. If that's the attention she wants, my guess is that she's getting it and more."

Ken started laughing. "So, not the girl you take home to mother?"

Brian was now smiling too. "Not unless you want mom to die of a heart attack. I think I'd worry more about the effect it would have on my dad."

Now Ken was really laughing. "Oh, geez!"

"No," Brian refocused, "I like Lisa. *That's* the kind of girl you take home."

"Her friend Autumn is cute," Ken observed.

"Yeah, but I hear she dates older guys. I think she's going with a junior at Canyon High."

"Too bad," Ken said. "I wouldn't mind double-dating with you some time."

"I have to get the date first," Brian replied.

"Are you going to ask her?" Ken asked.

"At the right time," Brian replied.

"In other words, you're scared," Ken shot back.

Brian was noticeably hesitant, "It's just a timing thing. I want to have it planned out." Brian's mom would often tease him when Brian would talk about dating girls. "Being that you don't have a driver's license or a job to pay for a date," she would ask sarcastically, "where do junior high kids go when they 'ask someone out'?" Brian would have to explain that they just hang out. That would warrant a, "So are you *hanging out* with anyone now?" And Brian would have to give his mother the patented junior high response of, *You just don't get it.*

CHAPTER 7

There was a knock at Wendy Swarengen's classroom door after school. Jeff Michael did not bother to wait for her to answer it. "Knock, knock," he said as he walked in.

"Hi, Jeff," Wendy said pleasantly, "What's happening in the P.E. department?"

Jeff Michael was the eighth grade P.E. teacher. His teaching career was going on seven years. Like most P.E. teachers, he was in pretty good shape. He loved teaching physical education and helping students stay healthy. He had expressed concerns to the administration many times about the growing problem with obesity in the students. It was not just a physical problem either. Overweight students constantly got ridiculed by their peers, which became even more frequent in P.E. class. Jeff hated how vicious the students got with each other. The sad thing was that the students who needed physical education the most were, many times, embarrassed to come to class.

Some of them would try to get their parents to allow them to opt out of the class. However, physical education was a required course in the state of California. So, many parents would talk their doctors into writing notes that would allow their children to be exempt from the class. They would falsely state reasons like asthma. These parents were attempting to "protect the self-esteem" of their children. In reality, they were perpetuating the problem. The obese child still knew he was obese.

"The P.E. department is doing fine," he replied. "The P.E. teacher is not."

"What's happening?" Wendy asked. She was at her desk preparing the next day's English lesson. Wendy was on her ninth year of teaching. When she saw Jeff's face, she could see that he was visibly upset. She stopped what she was doing.

"I'm thirty-one years old, I'm engaged to a wonderful lady that has expressed how much she wants to have kids, and the more I work with kids, the less I want to have any."

Wendy gave a little chuckle, "They're not *all* bad you know. John and I have two; they can be a handful, but we love them to death. It's different when they're your own. And by the way, the majority of the kids here love you. I've heard them say very nice things about you. They think you're fun, and they know you care."

"Did you see Jasmine Stone today?" Jeff asked.

Wendy's smile went away. "Are you talking about what she was almost wearing today?"

"Yep," he responded, "and I was dumb enough to tell her that she was dressed inappropriately."

"Why was that dumb?" Wendy inquired.

"Because that little tramp looked at me and said, in front of the whole class, 'Why are you checking me out?' Some of the kids gave some 'ooohs,' and I sent her butt up to the office."

"Well, I'm glad you did that," Wendy said.

"You know how these kids are. I don't need kids going home to their parents and giving their version of this."

"But you sent her up to the office. I'm sure Kim saw what she was wearing and took care of it."

Jeff continued, "Kim wasn't there. She got to see Carl. And you know he's not going to do anything about it." Carl Lane was the school principal. He had often expressed to the school staff that he did not want to be bothered with issues like students' attire.

"Oh," Wendy responded, "I get it. Well, if I were you, I would meet with Kim ASAP and fill her in. That girl is a major red flag. Kim knows that too. I have spoken to her many times about little Jasmine and her skimpy outfits." Wendy took a deep breath, "The fact is, we need a dress code here."

"Yeah, right!" Jeff shot back. "There is *no way* that Carl would go there."

"Yeah, I know," Wendy said. "I've already tried

to talk to him about it. He told me that he needs that headache like a hole in the head. But we really need it," Wendy said in a pleading voice. "I know the kids don't want uniforms, but what they're being allowed to wear is awful! Between the girls' bras sticking out, and the boys' underwear showing, I don't know what's worse."

"Now you see why I don't want to have one. I don't want to deal with that either," Jeff said. "I don't want to hear my kid saying, 'But, Dad, this is what everyone is wearing.' How do you control it?"

"I know how you feel, but they're not all like that," Wendy countered. "Look at Lisa Kaye or Brian Holm. Those are awesome kids, and they dress nice."

"Well, I can't argue with that. Those are really good kids. Their parents are nice people too. Brian is a good leader in my class." Jeff went quiet for a moment, and then he began again. "Wendy, I don't know if I want to do this anymore. I just don't support the system, and I feel like I'm compromising my values."

Wendy took that in. "I can't deny that I haven't felt the same. I often ask myself if I would want my boys here."

"Would you?" Jeff asked.

Wendy gave that a long thought. "No."

CHAPTER 8

It was after dinner hours at the Kaye house. Lisa was in her dad's home office working on her history paper. She had told her parents that she was really excited about doing this paper. Her parents wanted to know which historical figure she had selected to report on, but Lisa would not say. Her mother was doing last minute clean up in the kitchen. James had dinner with the family, but then he went out to help a family with their finances. He would be gone about two hours.

As she was cleaning up, Bethany was also listening to the T.V. It was an election year, and a political ad came on:

Senator Hopkins' views are too ridged for today's America. He wants to force Americans to be responsible for their own health benefits. He refuses to acknowledge gay rights. He refuses to endorse the banning of hand guns legislation. He voted against the removal of In God We Trust on currency and against amnesty for those who risked their lives to come to this country and work the jobs that Americans won't do. He rejects the scientific evidence of global warming. And he wants to take away a woman's right to choose.

The scene then changed to another man playing guitar on stage with a famous rock band on a popular teen music channel, and teen-age kids with their hands in the air cheering.

Governor Clayton knows how to reach out to every American. He is open-minded to all Americans' views. He supports a woman's right to choose. He understands our country is progressive, and that many things that were held as moral years ago, are offensive to some people now. Governor Clayton wants to ban guns and stop the killing in our streets. He wants to provide government health care to all Americans. And he wants to enforce stricter laws that would reverse the global warming that is quickly destroying our precious planet. Isn't that what's good for *all* Americans? Governor Clayton for President.

God help us if that idiot gets elected! Bethany thought to herself. She shut off the T.V. and walked out of the room.

~

It was Wednesday evening, and that meant that Lisa would be going to church to attend her youth group. She loved being involved with it, and she really liked Pastor Mike Davies. Before she had left, she called Autumn to invite her along. Autumn had politely declined saying it just was not for her. She had also told Lisa that she felt especially tired.

Lisa and her mom arrived at the church and went to their respective groups. Bethany enjoyed her adult Bible study group, and when James was not helping a family, he would join her. The nights he was not able to be there, Bethany would fill him in on the notes.

Lisa went into the room and saw her friend Tammy Ramirez. "Hey, Tammy."

"Hi Lisa," Tammy replied, "How's it goin'?"

"It's good. How about you?"

"Things are good here, but I've been really busy with school work."

"Speaking of school," Lisa began, "I never did ask you what happened with Ms. Wallace."

"Well, when I was in Mrs. Faretti's office, she asked me what had happened, and I told her the whole thing. I think she believed me too. At least she listens to us. She gave me the whole 'we-need-to-respect-the-teachers' stuff, and I told her that I didn't think I was being disrespectful. I told her that I felt Ms. Wallace doesn't respect other peoples' views, and every time one of us questions her views, we get in trouble. Anyway, I really didn't get in trouble. My parents don't like her, but they still gave me a warning to watch myself."

"I wish I had your nerve to stand up to her," Lisa said. "The whole class was silently applauding you and Brian—except Jasmine, of course. She believes everything Ms. Wallace says."

"She probably practices it too," Tammy shot back. She paused for a minute in thought and then continued, "Something interesting happened the next day though."

"What?" Lisa asked with curiosity.

"Ms. Wallace pulled me aside, and she got *really close* to apologizing to me. She said that even though she didn't like the outburst, she thought it was good that women learn to speak up for themselves."

"Do you think she had that conversation with Brian?" Lisa asked.

Tammy sarcastically laughed, "Are you kidding? She hates men. Can't you tell?" Lisa just stood there quietly. She thought that she was the only girl that had caught on to that. "Speaking of Brian," Tammy switched subjects, "That guy likes you."

Lisa's cheeks turned red. "No he doesn't," she said blushing.

"Yes he does," Tammy said back.

"Why would you say that?" asked Lisa.

"He watches you in class all the time. His eyes are so focused on you, and he always has a cute smile when he's looking at you," Tammy said.

Lisa could see that she was enjoying the conversation. "Has he said anything to you?"

"He doesn't have to. He'll be here tonight. Just keep an eye on him. You'll see." Tammy paused. "I think he's cute. If you don't want him, I'll take him, but I think he's stuck on you."

"My parents don't let me date," Lisa responded. "Besides, I don't know what he'd see in me."

"What are you talking about?" Tammy almost yelled. "Don't you think you're pretty?"

Lisa never really thought about it. Her dad always called her Beautiful and Dad's Gorgeous Girl, but she never really took him seriously. After all, it was her dad saying it. She thought Autumn was pretty, and Tammy was tall and slender with red hair. "I don't think I'm anything special."

"Girl," Tammy began, "you're pretty without even trying. Most of the guys at school don't notice you because they're too busy tripping over their tongues looking at Jasmine's butt cheeks. But a guy like Brian—one of the good guys—would never miss you. And I'm telling you, he likes you."

The subject felt uncomfortable for Lisa, and she quickly found a way to change it. "Oh, there's Pastor Mike. I need to ask him something. I'll talk to you later, Tammy." And Lisa quickly walked away.

Pastor Mike Davies had been the youth pastor at Road to Calvary Church for four years. He loved the kids—though he would never think of calling them kids in public—and they loved him. He was newly married, and like most youth pastors, he struggled to make ends meet. Once in awhile he would do some odd jobs on the side to bring in some extra money. But this is where his heart was, his calling. He saw Lisa approaching him and stuck up his hand for a high five. "Hey, Lisa," he greeted her with his perfect smile, "How are you?"

"I'm doing fine. I wanted to know if I could talk with you for a few minutes after group to ask you some questions on a history project I'm working on."

"Are you sure you want my opinion?" he asked. "I was a P.E. major before I started youth ministries."

"I think you'll be able to help me," she said confidently. "It's not that hard."

"Okay, I'll give you a few minutes."

Lisa said thanks and walked away happy. She happened to glance at the door when Brian Holm walked in. He gave her a big smile and started her way. Lisa's anxiety level went to a new high, and she quickly turned towards the rest room door. She walked in and locked the door where she tried to catch her breath. *Oh God,* she thought, *what should I do?* She stood there quietly for what seemed like a lifetime. Suddenly a knock came upon the door. She jumped back startled.

"Lisa, it's Tammy," she heard in a loud whisper. "You big wimp. I saw you run away. Get out here and talk to him."

Thank God I'm in the rest room! She thought. "No, I don't want to come out," she whispered back.

"Geez, girl! You can't stay in there all night," Tammy said with a laugh. "Just come out and be friendly."

"I don't want to talk to him," she said.

"Will you just come out here," Tammy ordered. "We'll sit on the opposite side of the room. It'll be okay."

Lisa opened the door and came out. Her face was red with fear and embarrassment. She felt like everyone was looking at her. She did not see Brian as Tammy and she walked to the chairs on the other side of the room. But as she was about to take her seat, she felt a tap on her shoulder. She suddenly turned and was looking Brian right in his blue eyes. "Are you okay?" he asked.

Lisa felt her knees buckle as she reached for the chair. Had Brian not grabbed her arm, she would have crashed and tumbled right over it. Tammy helped with the other arm. Lisa knew that everyone had to be watching her now, and she started feeling exceptionally hot.

"I've got her," Tammy said. "She'll be okay now. Thanks for helping, Brian."

"Is she okay?" Brian asked with sincere concern.

"She'll be okay," Tammy said, biting her cheeks to try to keep from laughing.

"Here," said Brian pulling up the chair, "let me get that for you."

"Thanks," Lisa managed to gasp.

Brian pulled another chair to himself. "I think I'll take this chair here and sit next to you, just in case."

Lisa saw Tammy's face. Tammy was doing everything she could not to explode with laughter. Her eyes started to tear from trying to hold it in.

"No, no," Lisa said, "It's okay. Go sit with your friends."

"Maybe in a bit. I just want to make sure you're okay," Brian said nobly.

Tammy could not take any more. She almost jumped up out of her chair. "I'll be right back," she said. She ran to the rest room with her hand over her mouth in laughter.

Oh, God! Lisa thought to herself, *She left me alone with him.*

"Can I get you some water?" Brian asked. There was an Arrowhead Water dispenser in the corner of the room.

"Really, it's okay," Lisa replied, "I'm fine. You don't need to stay here with me. Tammy will be right back."

Brian sat quietly for a moment, but he was not going to give up. "I like having you in my classes," he said, not knowing what else to say.

"Thanks," Lisa said, saying as little as possible to encourage him to go away.

"Who are you doing your history report on," Brian continued.

"I haven't decided yet," Lisa lied. *God, why won't he go away? And where is Tammy?* She thought to herself.

"You better get started soon. It's due Monday. I'm doing mine on Ronald Reagan. I read a biography on him. He was an awesome man!"

Lisa said nothing. Her palms were sweaty. Then she happened to look up, and from the other side of the room, she saw Tammy with another girl looking at her. Both girls had huge grins on their faces laughing. Lisa just wanted to melt. It was too much tension for her.

Brian finally said in a rejected tone, "Well, I was hoping to just get to know you a bit, Lisa. I'm sorry that I ended up annoying you. I hope you feel better." And with that, he got up and went to the other side of the room where Ken and some other boys were.

Lisa was relieved, but at the same time, she felt guilty. True, she wanted Brian to go away, but not upset. When she thought about it for a minute, she realized that he really was a nice guy—and cute. Everything was so . . . awkward. Lisa saw Tammy coming back towards her with a big smile on her face.

~

"How did it go?" Ken asked.

"Do I look happy?" Brian shot back. "I'd have better luck with a brick wall. She wouldn't even talk to me. Heck, I was just trying to be nice."

"There's always Jasmine," Ken threw in his usual

sarcasm. Brian glared at him with no response. "Dude, I'm joking. Look, man, I think she's just really shy."

"Whatever!" Brian exclaimed.

"There's other girls, dude. Don't sweat it."

Brian knew that Ken meant well, but he was not really good at saying the right thing all the time. At the same time, Brian was having a self-confidence issue—and a broken heart. By the end of the youth group time, Brian was looking forward to going home.

~

On the drive home, Lisa decided to consult her mother. "Mom," she began, "I need to ask you something."

"Sure, what's up? You sound pretty serious. Is everything okay?" Bethany asked.

"Well, something happened tonight that really made me feel uncomfortable."

Lisa told her mother the whole story. There were times when Bethany had to hold back her laughter for fear of offending her daughter and the fear of Lisa not wanting to open up again. *So, it's finally happened,* Bethany thought to herself, *Some smart boy finally realized how beautiful and sweet my little girl is.* "I know Brian's parents, Lisa. He comes from a really nice family. He's a nice boy. Do you think he was coming on too strong?"

Lisa thought for a moment. "No, I think it was more me than him. It just scared me, Mom. I've never had a guy like me before. And I don't know anything about guys. And now I feel bad because I know I hurt his feelings."

"You can fix that; you can apologize," Bethany replied. "Let me ask you something. Do you like him?"

Lisa was silent for a moment. "I don't really know him."

"Lisa, your dad and I think you're too young to date—"

"Mom, I never said I wanted to date!" Lisa interrupted.

"I know you didn't. Just listen for a minute," Bethany began. "Your dad and I were hoping that the boys wouldn't notice you for awhile longer. To us, you're our little girl. But you're not little anymore—and at the same time, you're not an adult yet. We kind of figured that because you're a bit shy, most guys would overlook you. But the fact is, you've become an attractive young lady, and guys are starting to notice."

"Mom, am I pretty?" Lisa asked. "Tammy said I was, but I never really thought of myself as pretty."

"Hey, you come from good-looking parents, so yeah, you're pretty," Bethany said in jest. "So, how do you feel about Brian?"

Lisa was hesitant. "He seems nice. Everyone likes him. Tammy said that if I don't take him, she will."

"Don't let that pressure you," Bethany gently warned her.

"No, I don't feel pressured. The truth is, I don't know

how I feel. I think he's cute, but up until tonight, I never really noticed that either."

"I think it would be good for you to have a guy friend—not necessarily a boyfriend—and Brian's a nice boy. I think you should talk with him a little." Bethany paused in thought. "I think you should also talk with your dad a bit too. Let him give you some insight on males."

"How do you think Dad will take all this?" Lisa asked.

He'll be scared to death, Bethany thought to herself. "I think he'll be fine with it. It will be good for him to know where his little girl is in her life. I also think he'll appreciate it that you value his opinion. One of the biggest fears a parent has is that their child will get to an age where they *won't* come to them anymore. This will be good for you and your dad."

CHAPTER 9

The next day, just before health class, Lisa waited outside the room for Brian to arrive. She was nervous and hoping this would go quickly and painlessly. As Brian approached, Lisa started to breath heavily and her hands began to sweat. Brian did not bother to look up at her. Lisa tried to say his name to get his attention, but nothing came out of her mouth. Her throat was bone dry. She swallowed and tried again. "B-Brian." It was a combination of a stutter and a whisper. Brian kept walking, and Lisa realized that he did not hear her. Lisa reached out and tapped his shoulder. He turned around and met her green eyes. "Brian," she said shyly, "ah, I ah, I wanted to say I'm sorry for last night."

Brian slowly responded showing little care, "No big deal." He turned and began walking in the room.

Somehow, Lisa managed to muster up the courage to

tap him again. She was shaking hard now, and her eyes began to tear. "Brian, I'm really sorry."

This time Brian saw the sincerity in her eyes. He could see Lisa trembling. "It's okay," he said gently. "I was just trying to get to know you."

"I know," Lisa responded with a tear rolling down her cheek. "I've really never had experience with guy friends before, and I was scared."

Brian smiled, "Sorry I scared you. I didn't mean to."

"I know. In fact, you were really nice. My mom says you come from a nice family too. I just wanted to apologize." Lisa started to calm down a bit, but she was still shaking. "I hope next time I'll do better."

Brian put a smile on his face after he heard that. "Would you like to meet at lunch time? Maybe we could have more time to talk; class is about to start."

Lisa's first thought was no. She was scared to death. "Well, I usually have lunch with Autumn Woods."

"I usually hang out with Ken. Do you want us both to come?" Brian had a semi-smile on his face that almost shouted out Pleeeeese.

Lisa wanted badly to say no, but for whatever reason, she said okay.

Brian's smile was huge now. He told her where he usually sits, and they agreed to meet. "Do you need a tissue before you go in the room?" Brian offered.

"Yeah, thanks," Lisa responded. Brian went in the room to the box on Ms. Wallace's desk. Lisa suddenly realized how thoughtful Brian was. *Maybe lunch time will be nice,* she thought. *All I have to do now is explain this to Autumn.* Brian came back with the tissue and handed it to her. "Thanks," Lisa said. "I probably look like a crybaby."

Brian looked directly into her eyes, "I think you look nice."

Lisa looked away shyly with a smile. She felt her whole body tremble. "The bell's going to ring; I guess we should go in," she said with a dry throat. Her attitude changed for a moment, "God, I hate this class!"

"You and me both," Brian agreed. They both walked in the room and took their seats.

CHAPTER 10

James was with a young couple helping them with their finances. Before he walked into any client's home, he would routinely pray that the appointment would go well, that the clients would see that he was trying to help them, and that they would want to be helped. It was the same old story for this young couple: Neither had had any financial education in high school or college; they both had student loans; they both had a car payment; they got married after college; they both got jobs that barely paid the bills; they got an apartment to rent; they financed their furniture with credit cards; and they now had too much month at the end of their money. In many cases, there were children involved too. Thankfully, this couple did not have that added pressure yet. James had seen this too many times. This young couple, in particular, had really opened up to James. They told him how in love they were when they got married a little over a year ago, but now they were fighting almost daily and the main topic of debate was money.

James could not understand how the schools and colleges could justify themselves about teaching so many topics but not addressing the simple rules of how money works. Like a doctor, James would go to a family, diagnose the situation, examine the documents, and prescribe a solution. This was one of those times when James was acting more like a counselor at first.

"I just want you two to know that you're not the only ones in this situation. I've been with many couples who were madly in love, but, unfortunately, their lack of financial education and the stress it caused slowly began to chip away at their entire relationship." He noticed the conviction on their faces. "Let me ask you two something: Do you still love each other?" Both replied to him affirmatively. "So my guess is that if I can help you relieve this financial stress, then you two can get back to being in love again. Is that correct?" They both smiled and nodded up and down, and soon they were holding hands.

James taught them some financial basics. He started with The Rule of 72, which simply shows how money compounds. He showed them how to eliminate their debt with a debt-stacking process. He then made sure that they were both properly protected with level, term life insurance, which is typically three times less expensive than the cash value type. The wife had commented about how simple these concepts were and wondered why they were never shown them in high school or college. "It's likely because those same people are in the same boat that you are," James explained. "Let me show you one more thing they may have overlooked showing you." James showed them the four ways that money is made—a job, being self-employed, owning a business, and being an investor. "The reason why your cash flow is so limited is because you've chosen to make your money as an employee. In other words, someone else has control over your income."

"No one has ever shown us any other way to make money," the husband responded. "We were told that when we got our degrees, we'd be able to get a good job."

"And that's the issue," James responded, "There's no such thing as a good job."

The husband and wife both looked dumbfounded. It was clear to James that no one had ever told them that before.

"But lots of people have jobs," the wife contested.

"Yep," James agreed, "and they're in the same rut you're in too."

"Are you saying we got our degrees for nothing?" the husband asked.

"No, not necessarily," James replied. "It's what you choose to do with them. You can both pursue your careers. But did it ever occur to you that you could make more money doing them as a business, instead of working for someone?" James saw the looks on their faces. It clearly had not.

"But we don't know anything about owning a business," the wife countered.

"Let me ask you this: If today you hit the lottery, let's say it was fifty million, what would you want your life to look like?"

"A nice home by the beach would be nice," the wife offered.

"I'd like a Lamborghini," the husband said with a smile.

"I'd like to travel more and help out our parents,"

"Yeah, that would be nice," the husband agreed.

"Did anyone ever bother to ask you that question in high school or college?

"No." they both answered.

"That's because in high school and college, they teach you that there's a career box out there somewhere that you're supposed to fit into once you have your degree. They tell you that you have to decide what you want to be, as opposed to what you would like your life to look like. Because if they asked you that question, you would have asked yourselves if your degrees would bring you that life, wouldn't you?"

"I never thought of it like that," the husband said.

"Folks, education doesn't end with a degree. You'll go much further with self-education." James suggested that they start thinking outside of the box. He recommended many books that would help them in these areas.

The young couple was grateful. They referred James to friends and family members. James left feeling good. He knew that he had made a difference.

CHAPTER 11

Brian was excited and nervous at the same time about having lunch with Lisa. He felt that he needed to have some words with Ken first. *Oh God,* Brian thought, *please tell Ken not to act like an idiot.*

"Okay," Brian began, "you promise you won't say or do anything stupid." It really was not a question to his best friend. In fact, it was more of a friendly warning.

"Gee," Ken replied with sarcasm in his voice, "lucky for you I *am* stupid, or otherwise I might be offended."

Brian felt badly. "I'm sorry, man. It's just that . . . you know . . . I really like her."

"Oh, I think you more than like her," Ken replied. "I'll be good; I promise."

Brian had known Ken for three years now. They were acquaintances at school, but three years ago they ended up on the same basketball team in their youth league. From there they became best friends. Brian was about five foot eight with dirty blonde hair and had a fairly athletic body for a fourteen year old. Ken, on the other hand, was about two inches shorter than Brian, dark black hair, and scrawny. They were different in many ways, yet they got along well.

~

"And why do I need to be there?" Autumn asked.

"Because I'm scared to death," Lisa replied. "Autumn, please don't leave me alone. Tammy did that the other night, and I made a complete idiot of myself. I don't know how to talk in situations like this." She thought for a minute. "In fact, you do most of the talking."

"Why me?" Autumn asked. "I'm not the one he has the hots for."

"The hots for! Autumn, please don't say that. I can't believe he even wants to talk to me."

"Why not?" Autumn contested. "Don't you think you're good enough?"

"I'm not good with guys like you," Lisa responded shyly. "Guys notice you."

"Lisa, you are way prettier than me; you just haven't figured it out yet," Autumn countered. "I just happen to know more about what guys want than you do." She paused for a moment. "Well, lunch is only twenty-five minutes, so I guess I can stick it out with you." Autumn grimaced a moment.

"Is something wrong?" Lisa asked.

"I don't feel good," Autumn replied. "I'm sure it's nothing."

"Just make it through lunch with me; then you can go home sick."

Autumn seemed to recover. "You know, you haven't told me something."

"What's that?" Lisa asked.

"Do you like Brian?"

Lisa felt that uncomfortable feeling go through her again. "I don't know. I mean, I like him; he's nice—"

"He's good-looking too," Autumn interrupted. "Not my type—he's too young—but he's cute. Do you think he's cute?"

Lisa's cheeks were a bit pink now. "Up until a few days ago, I hadn't really noticed, but now that all this has happened, I did notice he's cute." She was smiling with her face towards the ground.

"Oh geez!" Autumn exclaimed. "You're going to need my help."

~

A few minutes later, the four of them were having lunch at a bench in the lunch area. The conversation mostly consisted of their classes, teachers, and parents. It gradually began to change to dating thanks to Autumn. She asked casual questions while Lisa just listened. "Have you ever had a girlfriend before, Brian?" she asked.

Brian looked uncomfortable, "No, not really. I liked someone before, but she never noticed me."

"Who?" Autumn asked.

"Yeah, who?" Ken asked with unawareness.

"No one from school," Brian replied with an annoyed look on his face. "It was a girl at our church youth group."

"Who?" Lisa joined in.

Oh, great, Brian thought to himself, *now Lisa's asking too. And I told Ken not to say anything stupid.* "Remember that girl Cathy who moved away a few months ago?"

"Oh, yeah," Lisa responded. "She was nice. That's why she probably didn't notice you."

"Because she was nice?" Ken asked.

"No," Lisa said with a chuckle, "because she was moving."

Brian wanted this subject to end, but unfortunately, Ken kept it going. "I heard you're dating a high school guy, Autumn," Ken said.

"Yeah, Jorge Vergado," Autumn replied. "He's a junior," she added with a bit of arrogance.

"I know him," Ken said, "My brother is sort of friends with him. They all quadruple dated last weekend."

Oops! Brian thought to himself, *there just went stupid. Someone hurry up and ring the bell to class.*

"Last weekend?" Autumn responded. "Jorge Vergado?"

Ken was so busy eating his sandwich that he did not

realize that his foot was in his mouth. "Yeah, he plays on the football team; kind of buff dude."

Lisa looked up at Autumn and noticed the stunned look on her face. "Hey, Autumn, we have P.E. next. Why don't we start heading over to the locker room." She was gathering her things as she was talking.

Autumn was noticeably upset. Her eyes began to tear. "Yeah, okay," she responded softly. "Catch up to me." And she turned and quickly walked away.

"Nice!" Brian glared at Ken.

Ken had a clueless look on his face. He looked at Brian and Lisa both. Suddenly he put his hand to his head in realization as to what he had just said. "Oh, crap! Oh, man! Lisa, I'm really sorry. Please tell Autumn I'm sorry," Ken pleaded.

"I've got to go, Brian," Lisa said. "She needs me." Lisa ran quickly to catch up with Autumn.

"Dude," Ken looked at Brian, "I am so sorry! It didn't even . . . I didn't even think . . ."

Brian wanted to lash out at Ken, but he knew that Ken did not mean for that to happen. "Yep," Brian said disappointedly, "you didn't think. Well, at least you didn't upset Lisa."

"No," Ken replied, still upset with himself, "I just crushed her best friend. I guess we won't be doing a lot of double dating."

Brian gave a half smile, "I guess not. Hey, it's not

your fault the jerk was cheating on her—unfortunately, you happened to be the one to tell her."

"Autumn seems pretty nice too," Ken said. "She deserves better than that guy."

"We all have choices," Brian ended.

~

Lisa caught up with Autumn who was crying on her way to the P.E. locker room. "Are you okay?"

Autumn said nothing for awhile. Lisa put her hand on Autumn's shoulder. "Lisa," Autumn said with a sniffle, "what's wrong with me?"

"There's nothing wrong with you," Lisa reassured her. "Jorge is just a jerk."

"Or maybe I'm just a loser—and it felt really nice being told by Ken Schilling."

"Autumn, Ken felt horrible once he figured out what he said," Lisa told her. "He may not be the sharpest knife in the drawer, but he was sensitive enough to realize that he put his foot in his mouth. Besides, Jorge is the one you should be mad at."

Autumn started to cry harder. "I really liked him. I thought he really cared about me."

"Did you guys have a lot in common?" Lisa asked.

Autumn looked confused by the question. "I don't know . . . He was just good-looking, older—you know."

"I really *don't* know," Lisa said. "I mean, did you two talk a lot or have lunch together?"

Autumn was a bit annoyed. "No. We just kissed a lot, made out—what do you think we did?"

Lisa was trying to be careful now. Her best friend was really down, but at the same time Lisa had strong suspicions about what had gone on between Autumn and Jorge. Very softly Lisa said, "I think you probably did things that I wouldn't do."

Autumn's face showed anger. "Thanks a lot, miss goody goody! I'm sure in about five more years you and Brian might actually hold hands."

Lisa did not want this to turn into a cat fight. "Autumn, I care about you. You're my best friend. I hate what Jorge did to you. But let's face it, you really didn't know him. It's been all physical. I don't know much about guys, except for how my dad treats my mom. And their marriage isn't perfect all the time—I know you think my parents are like the Bradys." That brought a small laugh to Autumn. "But my parents are more like best friends. They know each other really well."

"Well, unfortunately, I don't get to see my parents together," Autumn said, "and when they are together, it ain't good."

"I know," Lisa acknowledged. "But that doesn't mean you can't find a good guy."

"There are no *good guys*," Autumn shot back. "They're all creeps like Jorge!"

"Brian didn't seem that way," Lisa said back.

Autumn took a deep breath, "No, he seems nice. Are you starting to like him?"

Lisa began to smile a bit. "Yeah, but I didn't realize it until just now." She thought for a minute, "You know, Ken's kind of nice—a little slow, but nice."

"He's not my type," Autumn said emphatically.

"I wasn't necessarily suggesting that," Lisa said. "I'm just saying that not all guys are like Jorge."

"So now you're an expert on guys?" Autumn asked with light sarcasm.

Lisa smiled, "No, but I'm willing to take the time to get to know them first. I think you should too." Lisa paused; she had a question she still wanted to ask Autumn. "So what really happened between you two?"

"I really don't want to talk about it now. Okay?" They went off to P.E.

CHAPTER 12

It was after school, and Wendy Swarengen had asked to meet with Principal Carl Lane. She knocked at the door, and Carl told her to come in.

"Hi Carl," Wendy said with a smile. "I know you're busy, so I won't keep you long. I just wanted to run something by you."

"Have a seat," Carl pointed to the chair. "What's up?"

"I wanted to talk to you about something you probably don't want to talk about," Wendy said.

"Uh oh, that doesn't sound good," Carl said with a grin.

"I would really like to see this school impose some kind of dress code."

"Nope!" Carl did not even give it a thought.

"Well," Wendy tried again, but this time with some assertiveness, "I would be willing to work out a plan, and even head up a committee, and take as much of the burden off you as possible."

"The problem is, Wendy, is that, when everything's said and done, it always falls back on me."

Wendy persisted, "But what if I—"

Carl cut her off, "Wendy, in all honesty, I could care less what these kids wear. It's between them and their parents."

"Carl," she tried again, "have you really seen what some of these kids are wearing? It's scary. There are girls that look like they belong on a street corner and boys with their underwear sticking out."

"Yeah and then there's those church kids with their little crosses around their necks. That's offensive too. There's supposed to be a separation of Church and State."

Wendy started to get angry, especially because of the last comment. She had heard many people fall on that false line. Anyone who has ever actually *read* the Constitution knows that no such statement exist, and that was never the intent of the Founding Fathers. It also annoyed her that Carl tried to compare wearing crosses with underwear sticking out. She gave it one last try. "Carl, aren't we supposed to be preparing the kids for college and the real world?"

"No," he countered, "that's high school's job. And if they want to do dress codes, they can knock themselves out. That's a headache I don't need. Wendy, I know you mean well, but no."

Wendy was frustrated. "Thanks for your time." And she left his office. *Doesn't anyone care about these kids anymore?* She asked herself. *You take God out of everything, and that's what you get. I don't know if I can keep doing this.* Her last thought sank in deeply.

CHAPTER 13

It was 10:18 P.M. East Coast time. Curt Woods was exhausted. His meetings were getting longer and longer, and his company's business trips were getting more frequent. This one was in Boston. He sat on his hotel bed taking off his shoes. He was also hungry, but his hunger for sleep was greater. He laid his six-four body back on the bed and shut his eyes just for a moment to catch his breath; and before he knew it, he was asleep. He had promised Dena and the girls that he would call them when he got back to his hotel, which he figured would be around 7:00 P.M. his time.

~

"Mom, when is dad coming home," Summer Woods asked her mother.

"Who knows," Dena responded with frustration.

"He was supposed to call tonight, but obviously he must be preoccupied," she said as she glanced up at the clock on the oven. It read 9:27.

"Mom," Autumn chimed in, "are you and Dad okay?"

Dena knew at some time this question would likely come her way in some form. She first thought about playing it down. But then she decided that her two daughters were not children anymore. They deserved an honest answer. "Autumn, things haven't been okay for a long time, and it may be time to deal with the inevitable."

"Are you two talking about divorce, Mom?" Summer asked with concern.

"We haven't officially talked about it, but the writing's on the wall. I think your dad may have other interests."

"You mean he's cheating?" Autumn almost yelled.

"I can't say for sure," Dena explained, "but I've suspected it. I know he has a new secretary, and since then, it seems to me that she screens his calls, including mine."

"That tramp!" Autumn yelled this time. "Guys are jerks! Why don't you go down there and slap the b----across the face!"

"Autumn, I said I don't know for sure; and watch your mouth. For all I know, she's a nice person. It's just a little coincidental that he hires her, and now he's on more business trips and in more meetings 'till all hours of the night."

"I'm getting in his face when he comes home," Autumn said.

"You'll do no such thing," Dena told her. "This is between your dad and me."

"It involves all of us," Summer said.

"It does," Dena agreed, "but not yet. Girls, even if he isn't cheating, I just don't know if there's anything left between your dad and me."

CHAPTER 14

James wanted to do something fun with his family for the weekend. He told them that he wanted to go down to San Diego and see the zoo. It had been a long time since he had been there—elementary school to be exact—and he wanted to just hang out with his family and have fun. Lisa asked if she could invite Autumn to come along, and James said that was fine. Chris took his IPod.

They drove down Interstate 5 in the big Escalade, the "family car." The conversation was very casual, but for the first time, Autumn became very aware of Lisa's family dynamics. She knew that the Kayes were fairly wealthy, but they did not act like the evil rich people that all the T.V. shows portray. But the salient observation she made was that the family was together, and they liked—no loved— each other. Autumn asked James what exactly he did for a living, and James explained his profession to her briefly.

"It seems like you should be really busy all the time,

but Lisa always tells me that she gets to see you every day. How is that?"

"That's really simple," James responded. "I made the decision a few years ago that I wouldn't work for anyone ever again."

"Oh," Autumn responded, "you inherited all this."

James let out a small laugh. "No, Autumn, I figured out that having a job is like being a slave, and I decided that no one is ever going to tell me when I can be with my family, when I can take a vacation or go to the zoo, or how much I'm worth."

Autumn went quiet in thought. She thought everyone had a job; that everyone worked for someone else. Mr. Kaye just seemed so relaxed.

The San Diego Zoo is an icon in downtown San Diego. It is one of the world's most well-known zoos. Recently, they celebrated the birth of a baby panda. A panda born in captivity was rare, so the zoo took special precautions about the amount of people traffic that went through that exhibit.

It was perfect weather for the zoo, and the animals were active and easy to see. Many times, Autumn would see Mr. and Mrs. Kaye holding hands like they were on a first date. Autumn could not think of a time when she saw her parents hold hands. For that matter, she could not think of the last time she saw them together. *I bet my dad is cheating!* she thought to herself. *Men are jerks!* And yet, she did not think that about Lisa's father.

The girls were by themselves looking at two hyacinth macaws, massive, beautiful blue parrots from Brazil. "Lisa," Autumn began, "do you think your parents love each other like when they first met?"

Lisa gave that some thought before she answered. "I don't know. I wasn't there when they first met," she gave a small grin.

"I know that!" Autumn shot back. "You know what I mean. Are they still in love, or are they just pretending to be?"

Lisa did not give that any thought at all. "My parents really love each other. They argue just like anyone else's parents, but I know they love each other. Some times it's embarrassing to watch them." Lisa paused for a moment. "I take it you're asking me that because your parents aren't like that."

"My parents are nothing like that," Autumn responded. "My mom thinks my dad is cheating with his secretary. She says everything is, and has been, coming apart."

"That's so sad," Lisa responded. "What do you think?"

"About my dad or all of it?"

"I guess all of it," Lisa said.

"I don't know if my dad's cheating or not—he probably is, because guys are such jerks!" she added. "But if my mom thinks they're coming apart, they must be."

"Autumn," Lisa began, "I don't think all guys are jerks, and especially not my dad. I think Jorge is a jerk, and I think there are some definite jerks out there, but not all of them. So far, Brian seems to be a good guy."

"Well, you haven't let him . . . " Autumn stopped herself.

"Let him what?" Lisa almost demanded.

"Never mind," Autumn responded.

Lisa changed her tone, "You know, I know that something big happened between you two, and I think I know what it is, so I'm just going to ask you. Did you have sex with him?"

Autumn stayed quiet for a moment. Her eyes began to tear, and finally she spoke. "It happened like this." She told Lisa about the night that Jorge came over and all that she could remember.

"Autumn," Lisa said with concern, "you could be pregnant."

"I'm going to buy a test kit tomorrow," she quickly responded. "I haven't been feeling right lately, and . . . I'm late."

Lisa's eyes became wide open. "Oh, my God! Are you going to tell your mom?"

"Are you kidding!" It was not a question. "For right now, this is between you and me."

"Yeah, but—"

Autumn cut her off. "Lisa, I mean it." Autumn paused for a moment. "Can we stop talking about this for now? I just want to enjoy the animals."

Lisa put her hand on Autumn's shoulder, "Yeah, we can drop it."

～

Later that evening, James had asked Lisa if Autumn had a good time. "Yeah," Lisa said casually. "I think she needed to get out and get away."

"Is everything okay?" James asked.

Lisa did not want to reveal anything to her parents that she and Autumn had spoken about. "Well, you know, Dad, her family isn't like ours. They're not really close. I think when she sees you and Mom together, she wishes her parents were like that."

"You've told me before that her parents aren't really home much," James said.

"No," Lisa continued, "they're not. And they're not together much either. I think Autumn really needs her parents."

"Is she in some kind of trouble?" James probed.

Lisa seemed to skip a beat, "No," she almost stuttered, "she's fine."

"You know, Mom and I really haven't tried hard enough to reach out to them. Maybe we could invite them over for dinner some time soon. Do you think they'd join us?"

Lisa thought about that for a moment. "That could be interesting. I don't know if they would; and I don't know if you'd find a time when they're together. It's worth a try though." Lisa wanted to change the subject. "I need to put some last minute final touches on my history paper and print it out." She discretely walked out of the room.

James walked into the office room where Bethany was working on one of her floral projects. James admired her creative talent—something he did not possess in an arts and crafts form. "I think something's up with Lisa's friend," he told Bethany.

"What makes you say that?" Bethany asked without looking up. James realized that Bethany was in an obsessive-compulsive state. When Bethany was doing one of her projects, there were very few things that could get her off focus.

"I was just asking her some questions about Autumn, and I felt like she was hiding something from me."

"Well, Dear," Bethany responded, "she is a teenager. There are going to be things now that she may not want to reveal right away." Bethany paused for a moment. "Oh, heck, I guess now is as good as time as any to tell you. James, your daughter has an admirer."

James was now the overly-focused one. The words went right through him. "I know she's a teenager and getting into the girly stuff, but she's always been able to come to me with anything. She's a great girl; there's a lot to admire about her." Suddenly, he heard his own words. "What do you mean she has an admirer?"

Bethany was now laughing. She told James about Brian. James actually pulled up a chair. "Oh God!" he exclaimed. "It starts. Why me, Lord?"

"I don't even know if the feeling is mutual yet," Bethany reassured him, "but at least it's a guy whose family we know."

"Do you think I should have a father-daughter talk with her?" James asked nervously.

"Why don't you give her a chance to approach you," Bethany suggested.

"Do you think she will?"

"I think she'll realize that she needs her father's wisdom," Bethany replied with a smile.

James smiled back.

CHAPTER 15

It was Monday morning, and Lisa was on her way to health class, the class she hated the most. But recently, it began to have an upside. "Hi, Lisa," Brian greeted her before they walked in the room.

Lisa drew a big smile, "Hi, Brian."

"Would you like to have lunch again today?" he asked. "I brought enough food to keep Ken from talking too much," he said with a smile.

"Yeah," Lisa actually responded boldly, "I'd like that. Don't worry about Ken. Autumn and I both know that he didn't mean to hurt her."

"He felt really bad about it," Brian added, "but he's a good guy when he's not eating his foot. Are you ready for class?" he motioned her towards the door.

"I hate this class," Lisa exclaimed.

"Me too; but it's getting more fun now that I get to talk to you."

Lisa blushed with a smile. *Yep,* she thought to herself, *I like him.*

Ms. Wallace had the title of her lesson on the white board at the front of the class, *How the Human Body Evolved.* She began to teach how the human body's internal and external organs and systems eventually changed through the evolution process.

A hand went up in the middle of the room. "How can anyone possibly prove that?" Tammy Ramirez asked.

"Through many scientific studies," Ms. Wallace countered.

The same hand rose up. "But evolution is a theory—and from what I've heard, a weak one."

"Ms. Ramirez," Ms. Wallace said with a calm but firm voice, "It is accepted as a scientific *fact.* It is the only *logical* explanation for our existence. All scientists agree that that is how it happened."

It was Brian's turn. "Are those the same scientists who don't believe in God?"

Ms. Wallace was turning red now. "Mr. Holm!" she shouted, "We will not go through this! These are scientific facts! We also will not discuss any religious matters in this class. The United States Constitution says there is a separation of Church and State."

"No it doesn't." It was a soft, unassuming voice. The students' heads began to turn towards it, and the looks on their faces showed surprise as to where it came from. Lisa was looking directly at Ms. Wallace as she said it.

"What did you say, Miss Kaye?" Ms. Wallace was glaring at her, and it was not a question.

Lisa did not cower. "I said the Constitution doesn't say that. It says that Congress cannot make a law that establishes a religion—it's the Establishment Clause in the First Amendment, and it never says that there will be a separation of Church and State."

"I am not going to have a debate with anyone today!" she said with a Clint Eastwood-style squint and her teeth together, "especially, when *everyone* knows about separation of Church and State. And the next out-of-line comment from anyone will land you at the office."

Lisa would say later that it was the strangest feeling she had ever had. It was a feeling of anger, fear, and determination all wrapped into one. She quickly jotted a small note, took her books off of her desk, stood up, looked Ms. Wallace directly in her eyes and said, "I know what the Constitution says. We study it more at my church than we do at this school."

Before Ms. Wallace could even open her mouth, Lisa handed a folder with the note she wrote to Tammy and headed towards the door. The note said *Give this to Mr. Norburg for me*. Ms. Wallace flicked the switch on the wall to tell the office that Lisa was on her way. As she was telling the secretary, she heard a voice say, "Tell them I'm coming too." And Brian Holm got up and walked out the door behind Lisa.

Ms. Wallace's face was pale when she turned around

and watched him leave. The rest of the students were in stunned silence. She opened the drawer to her desk, took out a piece of paper, and wrote a note. She stapled it and told one of the students to take it up. The outside of the note said *Attention Mr. Lane*.

~

Brian ran to catch up to Lisa. "Hey, wait up," he said.

"What are you doing here?" Lisa asked.

"I guess I couldn't keep my mouth shut either," he said with a grin. "I think the class is in shock. They couldn't believe you actually did that. I mean, no one would have expected it to be *you*."

"I hate that class; and I can't stand her!" Lisa said with strong anger. She then looked up at Brian, "We're going to be in serious trouble." She stopped walking for a moment, and her eyes became teary. She was slightly trembling.

Brian put his arm around her, "It's okay," he told her. For a minute, he could not believe that he actually had his arm around the girl he loved.

Unexpected to Brian, Lisa turned and put her arms around him. Her face was on his shoulder, and she said, "I don't want to go back in that class again."

Brian was now hugging Lisa. "I know how you feel. I don't want to either. I can't figure out how they let someone like that teach."

Lisa loosened her hold on Brian. She slowly pulled

away but did not move her head up to look at him. "She doesn't teach," Lisa said.

Brian felt now was as good a time as any, and he kissed her forehead. He had no idea what would happen next. But instead of backing up further, Lisa went forward and hugged him again with her cheek against his shoulder. Brian knew what he wanted to tell her next. He was just about to say it, when a voice called out, "Hey, you guys!" It was their classmate with the note. Lisa and Brian immediately let each other go. "This note is for you two. I have to give it to Mr. Lane. You two are way busted," he said.

"Crap!" Brian exclaimed. "I was hoping we'd have to see Mrs. Faretti. We *are* busted."

The three of them walked into the office together. The student handed the office manager the note and left to go back to class.

~

Carl Lane received the note from his office manager. He came out of his office and told Lisa to come in and take a seat. Brian started to stand up as well, but before he could, Mr. Lane sternly said, "You stay put! I'll get to you soon enough."

Mr. Lane closed the door and sat down behind his desk. "You're a real rebel rouser today, Miss Kaye," he said with a firm voice. "I take defiance very seriously—

especially when it is done publicly to upstage one of my teachers."

"I wasn't trying to—"

"Be quiet!" Mr. Lane quickly cut her off. "You'll speak when I tell you to. Ms. Wallace told me that an incident like this happened last week in your particular class period. It's obvious to me that last week's consequences weren't heavy enough to send a message to the rest of the class, so I will send it loud and clear today." He took out an official-looking piece of paper and began writing on it. "You're being suspended for public defiance in the classroom and failure to follow directions."

Lisa looked like she had just been hit with a tazer gun. Her eyes began to tear. "Can I tell you what I said?" she carefully asked.

"It's obvious to me that what you said practically turned Ms. Wallace's classroom upside-down," he answered. He looked at his computer screen to get Lisa's home phone number and then picked up the phone. "Hello, is this Mrs. Kaye? Hi, Mrs. Kaye, this is Principal Lane. I have Lisa in my office right now. . . No, she's fine; it's a discipline issue. Lisa decided to go off in Ms. Wallace's class today, and caused a major disruption, not to mention showed blatant defiance in front of the other students. . . Yes, Mrs. Kaye, your Lisa. Mrs. Kaye, this situation was bad enough to warrant a one-day suspension. I'm going to need her picked up at this time. Thank you. I look forward to talking with you shortly."

He put the phone down and addressed Lisa, "You can wait outside. Send your friend in please."

Lisa went out and told Brian to go into Mr. Lane's office. As she was sitting in the general office area waiting for her mother, Mrs. Faretti came walking in. Kim saw Lisa sitting there visibly upset. "Hi, Lisa. Is everything okay?"

"I'm being suspended," she said with a sniffle.

Kim did not expect to hear that. "For what?" she asked.

Lisa did her best to tell Mrs. Faretti the story. "Mrs. Faretti, is there any way I can get out of that class? I can't stand Ms. Wallace, and I'm not the only one."

Tell me something I don't know, kid, Kim thought to herself. "Health is a required class, Lisa."

"Isn't there anyone else that teaches it?" Lisa asked.

If there was, three quarters of the eighth grade class would be begging for a transfer, she thought again. "No, she's the only one. You hang in there."

Kim walked away and gave a tap on Carl Lane's door. He could see her through the glass. "Come in," he said.

"Hi, Mr. Lane," she said respectfully, "May I have a quick, private word with you?"

Carl's face showed annoyance, but he was careful not to act on it in front of a student. "Brian, could you step out for a moment, and do not go near Miss Kaye out there." Brian walked out, and Kim shut the door. "This better be important to disrupt a discipline situation."

That brought Kim's curiosity up for a moment. "I'm surprised I wasn't called for," she said. "May I ask why I wasn't?"

Carl tossed the note from Ms. Wallace in Kim's direction. She picked it up off the desk and read it. "Apparently, Ms. Wallace didn't feel like you handled the last situation well enough," Carl said.

"Carl, I would never second guess you in front of anyone, but I think you're making a bad decision suspending these two kids. These two are excellent students, and Wallace is not an easy woman to get along with."

"She's a veteran teacher, Kim, twenty years running. She knows what she's doing."

"Carl, she corners students with her 'my-way-or-the-highway' attitude. The kids can't stand her." She paused for a moment. "And to be honest with you, neither can I."

"Yes," he responded, "and that must have come out too in your last conversation with her, or I wouldn't have received that note."

Kim took a deep breath, "You're the boss; but I'm betting this could get worse before it gets better. Thanks. I'll send Brian back in." And she left his office.

CHAPTER 16

James was in his car driving to an appointment when he got the call from Bethany. "I'm sorry, Hun," he said, "For a minute there, I thought I heard you say suspended."

"I did say suspended," Bethany answered.

"*Our* Lisa suspended?" he asked as if Bethany was speaking a different language.

"Yes!" Bethany practically yelled. "Meet me at the school."

James called his client to inform him that a family emergency had suddenly come up. His client was fine with it, and they rescheduled.

About fifteen minutes later, Anthony and Linda Holm were having the same conversation about their child.

~

After her period of health class, Autumn Woods waited for her classmates to leave the room and then approached Ms. Wallace.

"Ms. Wallace, can I talk to you a minute?" she asked in a quiet voice.

"Sure, Autumn," she replied, "What is it? You look worried."

Autumn was extremely worried, and tears began to flow.

Ms. Wallace put her arm around her, "Autumn, what's wrong?"

"Ms. Wallace . . . I'm pregnant." she answered.

Ms. Wallace was taken off guard. "Oh, my!" she exclaimed. "Are you sure?"

Autumn nodded her head up and down, "I'm sure. I'm over a week late and I took a test. It came back positive. I don't know what to do."

"Have you told your parents?" Ms. Wallace asked.

"I can't," she said. "They'd kill me. I can't tell them this."

"What do you want to do?" Ms. Wallace asked.

Autumn paused, "I don't want to have a baby, and I don't want my parents to know. Will you help me?"

Ms. Wallace told Autumn to see her after school. She would make a phone call and see what she could do. "In the meantime, go to lunch, and don't discuss this with anyone else."

Autumn thanked her and said she would see Ms. Wallace after school.

~

When James arrived at the school, Bethany was already there. She was in the front office speaking with Lisa. Bethany told James that they had to wait for Mr. Lane because he was doing lunch supervision. Lisa explained the whole situation to her parents. After she was done, James and Bethany had the same confused look on their faces: *Why the suspension?*

"Lisa," James began, "tell me again what you told Mr. Lane about all of this."

"Dad, I told you—nothing," she replied. "Every time I tried to tell him what happened, he just cut me off. He told me to be quiet the first time I tried to tell him; and the second time I tried, he said he already knew what happened."

"So, you never got to tell him what you told Mom and me?" James clarified.

"No," Lisa affirmed.

"Stay here," he told Lisa. He pulled Bethany aside and spoke in a low soft voice. "This is *really* interesting," he began. "If she's telling the truth—and I have no reason to doubt it—then this principal really screwed up."

"How so?" Bethany asked.

"Well, before we go there, I just want to make sure that you and I are on the same page with things."

"Okay. Elaborate please."

"Look," he said, "when I was an assistant principal, parents would come in and fly off the handle about how their precious little angel would never have done whatever the heck they had done. I would hear the old, 'We-didn't-raise-Johnny-or-Suzy-that-way' story. Then, I would drop the bomb of evidence, and the poor parent would be sitting there looking like an idiot."

"So what you're saying is we need to be open minded to the possibility that our little angel hasn't told us everything," Bethany stated.

"Yep," James responded. "Look, I believe that she believes every word she's saying. I think she's being honest with us. But I've seen this situation before, and sometimes the teenage mind can forget details."

"Okay, so we'll be good listeners and nod our heads a lot," Bethany responded. "But there's something else you were going to say."

But before James could respond, the office door opened, and a tall, mid-fifty-year-old man came in. "Are you two Lisa's parents?" he asked.

James noted that he was smart enough to ask the question carefully. In today's world with divorce being so common, one could risk accidentally offending someone with the assumption of both having the same last name. James held out his hand, "I'm James Kaye, Lisa's father, and this is my wife Bethany, Lisa's mom." Bethany also offered her hand.

"I'm Mr. Lane. Why don't we step in here," Mr. Lane gestured to his office. "Lisa, I'd like to speak to your parents without you first," Mr. Lane told her.

Lisa just nodded her head up and down.

Carl Lane began telling James and Bethany the whole story and showed them Ms. Wallace's note. "So you see, Mr. and Mrs. Kaye, I can't let that kind of behavior in front of all those students go unpunished. I believe a strong message must be sent to the rest of the students."

"Where is Ms. Wallace?" Bethany asked. "I'd like to hear what she has to say about this."

"She has a class right now, but you can speak with her after school if she's available," Mr. Lane responded.

"That's probably not necessary," James said, which earned him a cross look from Bethany. "If you don't mind, Mr. Lane, I'd like to have Lisa come in for a moment."

Carl got up and opened the door and told Lisa to enter. Lisa sat down looking scared.

"Lisa," her father began, "I'd like you to go over again exactly what you told Mr. Lane about what happened in class."

Lisa looked confused. "Dad, I told you that I didn't get to tell him anything. I tried, but he wouldn't let me."

Carl took offense to that. "As I stated before, I already knew the story ahead of time; plus, it was a repeat of what had happened last week in her class."

"Did that happen last week too, Lisa?" James asked.

"Well, something similar happened, but I didn't say anything—it had nothing to do with me," she answered.

"The incident last week did not involve you?" James re-questioned her.

"No," she responded.

"This is some sort of trend that has been happening in this class, Mr. Kaye," Carl announced.

"Mr. Lane," James began again, "Do your discipline records on Lisa show that she was involved in that incident?"

Carl began to feel uncomfortable. "No," he answered.

"And is Lisa correct when she said that she tried to tell you what happened?" James kept his voice pleasant.

"Again, Mr. Kaye, as I said, this has become an ongoing problem."

James looked at Lisa. "Lisa, I want you to go out again please." Lisa got up and walked out.

"Mr. Lane," James began, "I asked my daughter to leave for a couple of reasons. First of all, I want you to know that my wife and I are not the type of parents that believe every word our daughter says. I will admit that I was shocked to hear that she was in deep enough trouble to warrant a suspension. Don't get me wrong, we have our battles with Lisa at home just like any other parents, but public displays of defiance are extremely out of character for her."

"Well, I—" Carl tried to cut in.

"Hang on, Mr. Lane, let me finish," James cut back. "With that being said, I want you to know that I believe *every* word my daughter has told us. I wasn't about to say that with my daughter here. I do agree that any form of grandstanding is inappropriate, though I don't think that was her intention. I can only go by what Lisa told me happened in the room, and that was a debate over Evolution being a scientific fact or a theory and separation of Church and State. If Ms. Wallace is going to teach on controversial subject matter, then she can likely expect controversy. According to Lisa, Ms. Wallace was presenting this to the kids as *fact*."

"Mr. Kaye," Mr. Lane cut in, "this is State approved curriculum."

"Maybe so, but that doesn't make it a fact."

"Well, the State isn't going to just approve anything," Carl countered.

"Mr. Lane," James responded, "that's neither here nor there. We all know that science has been wrong many times before—the world is flat; the earth is the center of the universe; the sound barrier cannot be broken— all these were considered facts, until someone proved otherwise. You and I both know there is no scientific evidence of Evolution. The State has called it a fact to keep people who support Creation quiet. However, my daughter attends a church that says otherwise, and that's the reason why she challenged it as a fact. Again, my point is that these types of topics *will* stir debate, and Ms. Wallace should know that. Wouldn't you agree?"

Carl stayed silent. He kept a poker face. "Mr. Kaye," he finally spoke up, "the problem here is that your daughter caused a big enough scene that other students joined in, and the learning environment was completely disrupted."

"That very well may be true," James agreed. "But what do you expect when someone is publicly challenging your beliefs and basically saying that's it and that's final?"

"You don't know that it went like that," Carl countered.

And that is when James became extremely focused. He looked Carl right in the eyes and said, "And that leads me to my next point: Neither do you."

Carl straightened up in his chair, "Excuse me?"

James leaned forward, "Mr. Lane, how long have you been a school administrator?"

Carl was becoming annoyed by this. "Mr. Kaye, I've been a school administrator for nine years now. I feel like I've been patient with you, but it's time to bring this to a close. You need to take your daughter home."

Bethany was watching this exchange begin to get heated up, and even she was wondering when it would come to an end. But she also knew her husband's background and figured he must be going somewhere with all of this.

"Not so fast, Mr. Lane," James shot back. "You see,

my daughter was absolutely right about the Constitution saying nothing about a separation of Church and State. She was also right about her learning more about the Constitution at her church then at this school. I know that because you have completely overlooked the Fifth Amendment requiring Due Process of Law. My daughter's Rights have been violated." James was practically glaring at him now.

Carl began to squirm in his chair. He looked very uncomfortable. "Mr. Kaye, I did no such thing," he countered, but his tone lacked confidence.

"You're a nine-year veteran, Mr. Lane. I purposely asked my daughter in front of you if she told you what she told us, and she said no, that she didn't get the chance to. And you acknowledged that, because—and I'll quote you—you 'already knew the story ahead of time.' Can you tell me where the Due Process is there?"

Carl Lane was in stunned silence for what seemed ten to twenty seconds. He stared at James and then attempted to relax himself. "Mr. Kaye, the Constitution and Ed. Code are two different things, and—"

James would have nothing to do with this, and he cut Carl off mid sentence, "That's right, Mr. Lane, and the Constitution is *The* Law of the Land." James stopped, and the room filled with uneasy silence again. "Mr. Lane, my daughter is not in this room, because I realized a while ago that you screwed up on this one, and I didn't want you to look bad in front of a student. But now, since it's just we three, I'm going to tell you how this is going to play out; and I think everyone will win here."

Carl's face was beginning to turn red, and his hands turned to fists. "Mr. Kaye, I think you may need to speak to our superintendent about this."

"Not a problem, Mr. Lane. Though I was hoping it wouldn't need to go that far, and I had no intention on dragging you through the mud."

Carl looked like a soldier that had to raise the white flag. "Go ahead. I'll hear you out."

James knew he had Carl's full attention now, and he had already worked out the angles in his head. He understood school politics, and appearance was everything. "Here's my plan: First, my daughter will not be suspended from school. I want any and all entries in her discipline records erased and a print out of her records to keep as proof. I have no problem with an entry that says you had to speak with her about disrupting the class, but the word 'suspension' will not appear. Second, I will allow you to suspend her from her health class for the day, and in all honesty, I would love it if she could be removed altogether."

"I can't do that," Carl responded. "It's a required class, and Ms. Wallace is the only one who teaches it."

James had figured that, but it was worth a try. "Fine, tomorrow, she will report directly to the office and quietly do whatever homework she has. I will make certain that she knows not to go near Ms. Wallace's class tomorrow.

That will allow you to show support for your teacher and allow her to have the appearance that she won the battle. And lastly, we'll have Lisa come back in, and I will tell her that I am in agreement with you that how she handled the situation was wrong; and that I support the class suspension. In exchange for that, I would like you to do some very careful monitoring of what is being discussed in that health class. To be honest with you, I do not like Ms. Wallace, and I do not support the State curriculum. I also believe—based upon some of the assignments that my daughter has brought home and what she has told me is discussed in class—that Ms. Wallace brings a lot of her own agenda to that class and tries to shove it down the kids' throats. So, I would ask that you review and observe what is being taught more closely. Fair enough?"

Carl nodded in defeat, "Okay, I'll go with that."

"Oh, one last thing," James said, "That boy out there waiting for his parents, we are close friends with his family."

Carl nodded. He took care of Lisa's discipline record and gave James a copy. Lisa was invited back in, and James stuck to his word. The adults shook hands, and Carl walked the Kayes out to the front door of the office. As they were walking out, Anthony and Linda Holm were walking towards them. "Hi, Linda," Bethany greeted her and gave a little hug. "What brings you here?"

Carl was watching the whole exchange between the two couples.

"We're here to see the Principal," Linda replied.

"Oh, Mr. Lane!" and Bethany gestured towards Carl. "We were just speaking with him," she said with a big smile. "Mr. Lane, do you know the Holms.?"

Carl held out his hand. "Hi, Mr. and Mrs. Holm. I'm Carl Lane, the principal here." They exchanged handshakes.

"What brings you here, Bethany?" Linda asked.

"Oh, we were just getting a copy of Lisa's records, and before we knew it, we got off on a long conversation about how important it is for all people to know and understand the Constitution. Anyway, we need to go. See you Wednesday night at church."

"Okay," Linda acknowledged. "See you there. Good to see you too James."

James gave a smile and a wave. He took a last look at Mr. Lane, who seemed to be choking on black feathers, and gave him a wave as well. Then he looked at his wife, "Ouch!" he said to her. And they walked to their cars.

CHAPTER 17

Autumn came to Ms. Wallace's room after school. She was packing her things up getting ready to go home. Autumn approached her and asked what she had found out.

"First of all, you need to know that the law states that you do not need to notify your parents to get an abortion."

Autumn felt relieved.

"Tomorrow, I'm going to take you to a clinic near by, but far enough away from the school, so you won't be likely to run into anyone you know. They'll take care of you there."

"Is this going to cost anything?" Autumn inquired.

"No, it's a free clinic," Ms. Wallace responded. "This will all be over tomorrow. But Autumn, we just covered a full unit on safe sex. I hope you learned something."

"I did, Ms. Wallace," Autumn said. "I promise this

won't happen again. Thank you so much." And she gave Ms. Wallace a hug.

~

The car ride home was semi-quiet, but when they arrived at the house, Lisa started asking more questions. "So I'm not suspended for the whole day?" Lisa asked with a degree of relief.

"No," James said, "not for the whole day, but you will be class suspended, and you are not to go anywhere near the room."

Lisa gave a small smile, "That's fine with me. Dad, is there any way I can get out of that class?"

James would have loved to been able to tell her yes. "No, health class is required. You'll have to endure. Just keep in mind what you've learned at church and home."

Lisa thought for a moment. "Did Brian get suspended?"

"I don't know," James replied. "That's between his family and the school. It really doesn't concern you."

"Well, he is my friend," Lisa said shyly.

That perked James up a bit. "I didn't know you two knew each other that well."

Lisa was a little reluctant. "Well, he's in two of my classes, and we go to church together, so we've gotten to know each other a bit."

"Just *friends?*" James pushed a bit.

"Well . . . I . . . I don't know, Dad," she managed to

say with a stutter. "We've recently begun to talk more, and I've realized I really like him."

James' heart was breaking. He was no longer the number one guy in his daughter's life. "I don't think you're ready to have a boyfriend, but I also know that I can't be with you every moment of the day, and I can't stop the inevitable."

"Inevitable?" Lisa asked.

"I knew some day some smart guy was going to notice my beautiful daughter," James replied. "I was just hoping it would be twenty more years from now."

"Dad! You keep asking me when I'm going to move out and stop being a burden on my parents," Lisa shot back with a smile.

"I was joking when I said that," he said. "I sometimes wish I could keep you forever, but that's not God's plan. I don't know Brian all that well, but he comes from a really good family. So if some *dude* had to notice my girl, I guess I'm glad it's a good dude," he said smiling.

Lisa was smiling, but she also became teary-eyed. "Dad, I love you and Mom. You'll always have me." She went over and hugged her father, and James' eyes became watery too.

A few minutes later, the phone rang. Lisa's mother told her it was for her.

"Hello."

"Did I hear correctly?" Autumn began. "You got suspended? Dang, girl! Even I've never been suspended.

Are you trying to change your good girl image over night?"

Lisa was a bit put off. "The news sure does travel fast. Who told you?"

"Tammy. She figured it out when you gave her your report and didn't show up for class after Wallace kicked you out," Autumn explained.

"I'm really not supposed to talk about it, Autumn," Lisa replied. "It's more of a class suspension plus the time I spent yesterday. That's all I can say."

"I heard how your boyfriend came to the rescue," Autumn teased.

"No," Lisa began, "I think he just got sick of Ms. Wallace too."

"I don't know what you have against Ms. Wallace," Autumn defended. "I think she's awesome. She's going out of her way to help me with a big issue."

"Oh, really? What?"

Autumn slowed down her response. "Now it's my turn to not be able to talk about it, but I'm glad she's there for me."

"Well," Lisa began, "since you asked. Ms. Wallace is constantly pushing her views on us, and I disagree with most of them. Haven't you noticed that anytime you disagree with her you get in trouble?"

"No."

Lisa felt a little dumb for asking, "Probably because you agree with her views."

"This must be one of those Christian things," Autumn said with a bit of sarcasm.

Lisa did not like it, "Yeah, it is. And if you knew the Lord, you would understand."

"I believe in God!" Autumn shot back.

"So does the devil," Lisa replied. "There's a big difference between believing in God and knowing Him. Though I must say, you're probably one step ahead of Ms. Wallace."

"I like her," Autumn said. "I think she's a good person. She's one adult that I feel comfortable talking to."

Lisa wanted to end the conversation. "Well, I'll see you tomorrow."

"Are we doing lunch with the boys?" Autumn asked.

"I'd like to . . . if you don't mind," Lisa said.

"It's fine with me. You really like him, don't you?"

Lisa smiled, "Yeah, I do."

CHAPTER 18

Bethany was reading in the office area. James came in to see what she was up to. He put his hands around her neck and gave her a little massage. "Oh, I needed that," Bethany exclaimed.

"Is your neck hurting?" James asked.

"I think it's tension. In spite of the fact that you were brilliant at the school today, it was stressful," Bethany replied. "James, should we have Lisa in a public school?"

"It's funny you should mention that," he said. "I was wondering the same thing. It's not like we can't afford a private school. Is this something you want to talk about with Lisa?"

"I think we owe that to her; after all, it will affect her the most."

"Let's have a family discussion this weekend. Chris too?"

"I don't think the values at his school are much

better," Bethany replied. "Yeah, I think it should be a family discussion."

Before James had walked in on Bethany, he was checking some of the sports scores on T.V. James always told his friends that he bleeds Lakers' purple and gold. It had been a good season for the Lakers finally. Kobe learned what it takes to be a leader. A commercial came on the screen:

Governor Clayton wants to stop the hatred that is building up in our public arenas—schools, courts, work places, and colleges. He believes it is time to stop the hate speech against minorities and those who want to live alternative lifestyles. "We don't need bigots and right-wing fanatics destroying our society. It's time to prosecute these people who defile our society." Vote for Governor Clayton this November. Stop the hate.

"Someone needs to expose that jerk for who he is," James said.

"Do you think he can get elected?" Bethany asked.

"Yep," James replied. "This type of thing is a direct attack on Christians. Can't you just see it: Pastor Jack one morning starts preaching out of Romans about homosexuality, and the 'hate crime police' come rushing in to take him away. That's what this is all about."

"Come on, James," Bethany said doubtfully, "this is America, not Nazi Germany."

"Really," James countered. "Did you know that it's a crime right now in many European countries?"

"No," Bethany said.

"In fact, did you know that in Great Britain they stopped teaching about the Holocaust, so they won't offend Muslims?"

"I did hear that one," Bethany replied. "They're trying to push God out, aren't they?"

"Yep. And they're trying to disguise it as *tolerance*."

"Oh, I see," Bethany said, "they'll tolerate anything except God and Christians."

"You got it," James said.

A couple minutes later, the phone rang. James picked it up. "Hello."

A young male voice spoke back. "Ah, hi, Mr. Kaye. Can I speak to Lisa please?"

"Who is this?" James asked.

"This is Brian Holm."

Oh, God! James thought, *She's getting calls now.* "Hang on a minute, Brian. I'll see if she's available."

Bethany heard the name and began to smile big. James called Lisa to the phone.

Lisa picked up, "Hello."

"Ah, hi, Lisa. It's Brian."

Oh my God! Lisa thought with excitement. "Hi."

"Are things okay?" Brian asked.

"You mean about today? Yes," she replied. "How about you?"

"It could have been worse," he said. "I'm suspended from class tomorrow—not that I care."

"Well, I guess I'll see you at the office fourth period."

"Oh, then it's not so bad after all," he said positively.

Lisa paused and thought for a minute before she spoke again. "Thanks for being there for me."

"It wasn't just for you," Brian responded. "I'm sick of her. I'm tired of the crud she throws at us."

Lisa realized that he did not get what she was saying. "I was actually talking about after we got kicked out—in the hall."

Brian caught on, "You're welcome. I enjoyed being there for you. Would it be okay if I was there for you again?" he held his breath after the question.

Lisa had a huge smile on her face now. "Yeah, I'd like it if you were there a lot." There was a long silence. "Do you want to have lunch again tomorrow?"

There was no hesitation, "Yes!" he almost yelled. "Do you mind if Ken is there?"

"No," Lisa answered. "And I've already invited Autumn."

"That's cool. I'll tell Ken not to say anything."

"Like I said, it wasn't his fault," Lisa said. "Autumn just happened to find a jerk. Right now, she doesn't believe there are any good guys out there. But I told her that I know of at least one."

Brian was feeling great all of the sudden. "Thanks," he said.

Lisa decided to have some fun. "I was talking about my dad," she said with a laugh, then quickly corrected herself just in case Brian did not know she was joking. "I'm kidding. I think you're one of the good ones."

"I think you're great," Brian said back.

Lisa's smile got even bigger. "Thanks. I'll see you tomorrow."

"Okay. Sleep well."

"You too. Goodnight."

Lisa was getting ready for bed. As she sat on her bed, she bowed her head to pray. "Lord, I thank you for watching over me today. Thank you for my family. I pray you'll watch over all of us. God, I thank you for my friends. I especially want to pray for Autumn. Lord, I just ask that you change her heart. I don't know what it will take for her to come to know you, but I pray that she will realize just how much you love her. Thank you for putting Brian in my life too, Lord. I pray he'll sleep well tonight. Lord, I guess I'm supposed to pray for Ms. Wallace too. I really don't like her, but I know I'm supposed to pray for her. I pray she will find salvation. In Jesus' name I pray. Amen."

CHAPTER 19

The school day was fairly routine, as far as classes went. Lisa and Brian spent fourth period in the office, and that was fine with them. They spent lunch with their friends, and Ken managed to not offend anyone. He took no time to sincerely apologize to Autumn who thanked him. Lisa was looking forward to seeing her grade on her history report, but Mr. Norburg had already warned the students that it would be at least a week before they received their papers back.

After school Lisa met with Autumn. Lisa told her that her mother was coming to pick her up and asked if Autumn wanted a ride home. "No, that's okay, Lisa. I'm, ah, meeting with Ms. Wallace after school. She's helping me with health stuff."

Lisa looked at her with an odd expression. "You need tutoring in *health*?"

Autumn did not want to arouse Lisa's curiosity in any way. "I just had a few questions for her; nothing big."

"Okay," Lisa said walking the other way. "Call me tonight."

"Will do." And Autumn headed towards Ms. Wallace's room.

She opened Ms. Wallace's classroom door, and Ms. Wallace was gathering her personal belongings. Without looking up, Ms. Wallace said, "Ready to go?"

Autumn, for the first time, felt an eerie feeling come over her. Her heart began to pound hard. She did not know what to expect. It finally occurred to her that this was very serious. "I'm ready, I guess. Is this going to hurt?"

Ms. Wallace never looked up. "I don't know. It may. After all, they are going to be dealing with a tender part of your body. But the bottom line is that you're fourteen, and you're not ready to be a mother. We're saving you a lot of grief."

Ms. Wallace turned off the lights in her room, and they walked to her car and left the school.

There was very little conversation on the way to the clinic. When they arrived, Autumn could not help but notice that it looked nothing like a hospital, just a small, one-story building. She went inside and took a seat. There was another teen-age girl and her mother seated in the waiting area.

"Mom, I don't want to do this. I don't want to kill a baby or go through this," the girl whispered audibly.

"You *will* do this!" her mother whispered a bit louder. "I will not have my unmarried daughter pregnant at age fifteen! You'll ruin your life! And I already raised my own kid; I'm not going to raise yours too. I'm too young to be called grandma!"

Autumn filled out the paperwork with Ms. Wallace's help and waited for her name to be called.

~

Curt Woods was in another long meeting. He would be at work very late—again! Dena Woods would not be home until 6:00 or 7:00 p.m. She just assumed, as usual, that her daughters would take care of their own dinner and take care of the house. Neither of them knew that their fourteen-year-old daughter was at a small clinic with her teacher going through a traumatic event.

~

When it was over, Autumn was in severe pain, in spite of the pain medication she was given. Ms. Wallace drove her to her house and helped her inside. She lay Autumn on the couch and told her to get some rest. It was 4:35 in the afternoon.

Summer Woods came into the house a little after 5:00. She saw her sister on the couch asleep. "Get up, you bum," she said to her incoherent sister. Autumn did not wake. "I'm not making you dinner." Summer gave Autumn a nudge, and Autumn groaned. "What's up with you?"

Autumn thought of the only excuse that made sense, "I have really bad cramps. Will you help me upstairs?"

"Geez!" Summer exclaimed, "You look like hell." She helped her sister off of the couch and up the stairs to her bed. Autumn quickly fell back to sleep.

The next morning her mother knocked on her door and yelled at her to get up. Autumn had no intentions on going to school. She felt terrible. Her mother finally opened the door, "Get up! You're late."

Autumn replied in a weak voice, "Mom, I can't go. I'm in so much pain. I've got really bad cramps."

Dena could see that her daughter was in pain, and she did not bother to push the issue. "Get some rest. I'll let the school know. I'm leaving for work; call me if you need anything." And Dena left Autumn in bed.

CHAPTER 20

Jeff Michael arrived at the school early, as was his routine. He found a note in his teacher's box that said, *See Me Immediately, Carl*. Jeff went into the main office and saw Carl Lane's door open. He gave it a slight knock and held up the note. "You need to see me?"

Carl looked up at him, "Come in, Jeff, and close the door."

Jeff did not like the tone, and he especially did not like the "close the door" part. He closed the door and sat down. "What's up?" he asked.

Carl picked up a small note. "You have a student named Jasmine Stone in your P.E. class." It was not a question.

"Yeah," Jeff acknowledged.

"Well, I just got off the phone with her mother. Her mom says that Jasmine is very uncomfortable around you, because she thinks you are checking her out. Her mom went as far as to call you a pervert."

Jeff was annoyed but calm, "And what did you tell her?"

"I told her that I would bring you in first thing and discuss this. I also told her that it might be a good idea to move her out of your class, which she agreed," Carl explained.

Jeff was getting upset fast. "Well, it sounds like you got it all worked out. Thanks." And Jeff began to stand up to walk out.

Carl was annoyed by his action and attitude. "Sit down," he ordered calmly, "I'm not done."

"I am," Jeff answered back. "I have nothing more to say. You've already confirmed with her mother that she is right."

"Just wait, Jeff," Carl said. "I never implied that I believe either the girl or her mom. I told her that I would look into this."

"And that you would move her out of my class, based on the notion that she believes I'm checking out her daughter," Jeff said back. "Look, Carl, in all honesty, I could care less if the girl stays in my class or not. She doesn't do anything anyways. Did you see her grade?"

"No," Carl replied, "I hadn't gotten there yet."

"She's failing; and she's getting a U in Citizenship." The students' Citizenship grade was based upon attitude and behavior. A "U" stood for Unsatisfactory. "In case you haven't figured it out, it takes a lot of doing nothing to fail P.E. And why? More than half the time she doesn't dress out—which, by the way, if she did, she'd be wearing more clothes than when she doesn't dress out. By the way, have you ever met her mother?"

"No," Carl said listening carefully.

"Why don't you invite her here for a conference? But if you do, be sure your door stays open. Let's just say the nut doesn't fall far from the tree."

Carl took it in, "Well, it sounds to me that it would be a good idea to move her out of your class."

Jeff took a deep breath and collected himself. "Carl, that's fine with me. In fact, I'd probably get better performance from the other kids, especially the boys, since they wouldn't be getting distracted. Here's the thing: I would have liked it if you would have told her that the three of us need to meet to discuss this and then made the decision. I would have suggested it. Right now, I don't feel supported by you.

"Jeff," Carl said calmly, "I support you. You're doing a good job."

Jeff was lightening up. "Carl, you say you do, but in reality you don't. The teachers here have expressed great concern about the lack of dress standards."

"I won't do it, Jeff," Carl cut in. "It's an administrative nightmare."

Jeff was sympathetic, "Carl, I'm sure it is. But a dress

code isn't just for the kids; it's for us too. Let me ask you this: Do you know who Jasmine is?"

Carl's face showed a little embarrassment, "I'm not sure. I've heard the name. There are a lot of kids here."

"I think you should invite her in here and meet this girl. But I have to warn you; try to keep your eyes from wandering. If this girl could walk around here naked, she would. I'm sure Kim knows her well. Carl, she looks like she should be at the corner of Hollywood and Vine—and her mother looks about the same. Little girls like that like to draw the wrong kind of attention to themselves. The problem is, *everyone* is looking. And if it's someone they don't like, well that person must be a pervert or child molester. If she wasn't allowed to dress like that here, you and I wouldn't be talking right now."

"I won't do the dress code thing, Jeff," Carl said. "This office will be packed with students everyday."

"Yeah, but if we enforce it, the kids will catch on, and it will stop."

"It won't stop," Carl disagreed. "It will be less frequent, most likely, but it won't stop. Then you'll get the teachers making judgments on students' clothing, and then you'll be begging for my support."

Jeff felt defeated, "Then I don't know what to tell you. But I will say this: I'm not going to stand around and let some little tramp and her mom destroy my reputation or get some rumor going around with the students. I'm a teacher, and I can't afford lawyers' fees."

Carl had heard enough as well. "Let's give her mom a call right now. I'll hand the phone off to you and let you tell her that you feel it's in everyone's best interest that we take her out of your class. You can tell her that the accusation is false, but you feel that her daughter may do better with a change. Does that sound okay?"

Jeff was worn out too. "That's fine," he said. *What a way to start the day,* he thought to himself. *And the hits just keep on playing!*

CHAPTER 21

Lisa was a little disappointed that Autumn was not at school. Autumn seemed fine yesterday. It made a couple of her classes a little boring. Lisa told herself to give Autumn a call when she got home today.

Mr. Norburg addressed the class by again stating that he was still correcting their essays and not to ask about them. "Today we are starting a new unit. As all of you know, the world has changed since 911. And because of that, groups of people are being judged based upon their beliefs. Well, this is America, and all religious beliefs are welcome. This unit is going to be on Islam, a religion of peace. And what we will be studying is the Islamic culture and the history of the Muslim people." A hand went up. "Yes, Miss Ramirez."

"I'm curious, Mr. Norburg," Tammy began. "Will we be studying other religions as well?"

"Probably not," Mr. Norburg answered. "Islam is,

sort of, new to the United States, and with all the bad impressions people got from a select, radical few, many schools have decided it would be a good idea to stifle the stereotype and bias that's out there right now—especially being brought out by other religious groups. This also falls under the State's commitment to promote cultural diversity."

"What do you mean by bias from other religions?" she asked with a perturbed voice and facial expression.

"There are other religions out there that believe that Islam is bad and Muslims are evil, and that they have the market on God. Now I don't want to get into a religious debate here. This is going to be about understanding a different culture." He picked up a stack of pamphlets and began passing them out. "These are pamphlets that were given to us by local Islamic leaders which were meant to educate. We may even get lucky enough to get a couple of them here to speak to you." Mr. Norburg told the class that there would be art projects to get involved in, dressing up, and that the class would be learning verses from the Quran.

After class, Lisa approached Tammy. "What do you think?"

"I think my parents would have a cow with this," Tammy answered. "Do you honestly think they would be making a big deal about Christianity?"

"No," Lisa responded. "And if they did, every protester and Christian hater would be here yelling."

"I'm not reading the Quran. We've already heard verses out of it that tell them to kill the non-Muslims. No one is going to convince me that this is a religion of peace."

"I'm with you," Lisa said. "My parents won't like this either."

CHAPTER 22

When Lisa arrived home, the first thing she did was call Autumn. Autumn answered the phone in an agonizing voice. "Hello."

Lisa did not expect to hear her friend in such pain. "Wow! You sound terrible. What's wrong?"

"I'm in a lot of pain," she answered. "I . . . ah, have really bad cramps."

Something told Lisa that it was more than that. "Cramps? You sound like you're dying. Is anyone with you?"

"No," Autumn said. "My mom is at work, and my sister is spending the night at one of her friend's house. My mom called awhile ago and said she had to work overtime. And my dad is on another one of his business trips."

Lisa was hearing her friend's voice, and she could feel deep inside that there was something more to

Autumn's ailment. "Autumn, what's going on? I know this isn't cramps."

Autumn was hesitant. There was a long silence. "I don't want to tell you," she finally answered.

"Autumn, we're best friends. If you can't tell me, who can you tell?" Lisa decided to ask what she wanted to ask, "Are you pregnant?"

Again, there was a long silence. Finally, Autumn answered, "Not anymore."

Lisa felt a chill go through her body. *Oh, my God!* she thought to herself. She could not think of anything to say. She finally came up with the only thing she could think of: "Have you eaten?" Lisa asked.

"Gosh, I've been in so much pain that I didn't realize how hungry I was until you mentioned it."

"Why don't you come over for dinner with us?" Lisa invited.

"I don't know," Autumn said. "I feel like hell."

"I don't doubt it," Lisa affirmed, "but you need a friend right now."

"Is it okay?"

"I know my mom; it's fine. I'm sure we can come get you too."

"Okay. In all honesty, I don't feel like getting out of bed, but I would like to be with you. I'll get myself dressed. Lisa, don't tell your parents."

"Okay. We'll be there soon."

On the way to Autumn's house, Lisa told her mother

about the lesson on Islam that she was required to study. Bethany was not happy; "Nope!" she said emphatically, "No one is going to *make* my daughter read the Quran. They would never tolerate the Bible being read, and they'd never allow Pastor Jack to come in and talk about Christianity. I'll have to give the school a ring on this one."

Approximately twenty minutes later, Lisa and her mom arrived at Autumn's house. Lisa went to the door to get her and noticed that Autumn was moving extremely slowly. "Hi," Lisa said and gave her a hug. Autumn was a little off balance, but she hugged her friend with a smile. Lisa helped her walk to the car and get in.

"Autumn," Bethany began, "you look awful. Are you okay?"

"Hi, Mrs. Kaye," Autumn said. "I'll be okay."

"You can relax at our house and then have dinner," Bethany told her.

"That sounds good," Autumn replied.

Bethany was worried about her daughter's friend. *Where the heck are her parents?* she asked herself. Lisa had already told her where they were. Bethany suddenly began to think about the decision—or as some of their friends and family told them, the *risk*—that she and James had made to start and build a business. Their jobs would have never allowed them to be there for their children. And now here she was, taking care of someone else's. But that is why they paid the price then; so they could have their lives back now.

As the ladies pulled up to the house and got out of the car, they could smell the aroma of a barbeque. James had already begun cooking the steaks. "I'm hungry now," Lisa said.

"That smells great," Autumn agreed.

Twenty minutes later, James, Bethany, Chris, Lisa and Autumn were having a meal together. As they ate, Bethany noticed that Autumn was struggling to sit up in her chair with out grimacing from pain. After dinner, James went out to clean the grill. Bethany told Lisa and Chris to help her with the dishes. "Autumn," Bethany said, "Why don't you go lie down on the couch. We'll take care of the dishes."

Autumn got up and began walking towards the living room. She was half way to the couch when she collapsed. Lisa saw her friend fall down and called her mother. Bethany ran over to Autumn who was unconscious. "James!" she yelled. "She passed out! Lisa, call 911."

Lisa ran to the phone and made the call. James and Bethany checked Autumn for a pulse. She had one and was breathing as well. "Chris," James said, "Help me get her on the couch. Keep her as straight as possible."

"We need to contact her parents," Bethany said. "Lisa, do you have any way of getting hold of them?"

"I only have the home number," Lisa replied.

"Call the home and leave a message on their recorder," James told her.

Lisa dialed the home number and heard a disturbing

message: "The mailbox is full. Please try your call later," the machine told her.

"Mom, the mailbox is full. I can't leave a message."

"Write down the number, so we can call from the hospital."

Lisa thought for a minute. "Mom, I know Brian lives near her. Maybe he can put a note on the door."

"Call him up, and tell him to put a note on the door saying there's been an emergency. Give him my cell number to put on the note. Don't give details, Lisa. Just tell him to make sure the note is big enough to see."

"I'll take care of it," Lisa assured her. Lisa called Brian's house. His mother answered, and Lisa asked to speak to him. Lisa heard a siren in the distance approaching.

Brian came on the phone. "Hello."

"Brian, it's me."

Brian was pleasantly surprised. "Hi. What's happening?"

"Brian, I need a huge favor. Autumn lives down the street from you, right?"

"Yeah," Brian confirmed. He could hear the panic in Lisa's voice. "Is everything okay?"

"Brian, Autumn is really sick. She's over my house right now, and the paramedics are on their way. I tried to call her house to leave a message for her parents when they come home from work, but the answering machine is full. Do you have a pen and paper handy?"

"Yeah."

"Put a big note on their door telling them there's an emergency, and have them call my mom's cell number. Here it is." Lisa told him the number and asked him to call it when he had finished.

"No problem!" Brian said. "I'll call you in about ten minutes."

"Thanks, Brian. Oh, pray for Autumn."

"I will—and you too."

That gave Lisa a brief smile. "Thanks."

The paramedics came to the door. They began examining Autumn. One said to another that Autumn's blood pressure was low. Another paramedic began asking Bethany and James questions about Autumn, but neither of them had good answers. Lisa finally spoke up, "She had an abortion yesterday."

James and Bethany looked like they were in shock. Before they could speak to Lisa, the paramedic began asking her questions. "Do you know where she went to have it?"

"I only found out three hours ago. She hadn't told me anything yet." Lisa turned to her parents. "Mom, I was hoping that after dinner the three of us could talk, and Autumn would have felt comfortable enough to tell you. I was going to tell you even if she didn't, but then this happened." She had tears in her eyes now.

"Did she say anything else you can think of?" the paramedic asked.

"No, but I think Ms. Wallace, our health teacher at school, may have been the one who took her."

"Why would you think that?" James asked.

"Yesterday, she told me that she was meeting Ms. Wallace after school for some extra help."

"Has anyone tried to reach her parents yet?" the paramedic asked.

"We're working on that," Bethany said. "So far, no response. Both of the parents work. We have friends who live near by her trying to contact her parents."

As this discussion was taking place, the other paramedics were still examining Autumn, who was wearing tan sweat pants. The female paramedic said she noticed a blood stain at the crotch of the pants. The third paramedic told the others that Autumn was good to transport.

"I'm going to follow the ambulance," James told the family.

"Dad," Lisa said, "I want to go with you."

"You have school tomorrow," James said.

"Dad, I feel—"

Bethany cut in, "It's okay, James. She can go, and she can miss tomorrow if necessary. Chris and I will stay here and man the fort. Lisa, you gave Brian my number, right?"

"Yes."

"James, when you get to the hospital, make sure you find a phone there that I can call in case you can't get a signal on your cell. I'll come by in awhile and bring some snacks. Meanwhile, I'm going to keep trying to reach someone at the Woods' house."

"Sounds good," James agreed. And he and Lisa left for the hospital.

CHAPTER 23

Brian made a sign on 8 ½" x 11" paper. He took some tape with him and quickly jogged down the street to the Woods' house. He then taped the sign to the front door and went home and called the number Lisa had given him. Bethany thanked him.

"Is Autumn going to be okay, Mrs. Kaye?" Brian asked.

"I don't know, Brian. They took her to the hospital," Bethany replied.

"Can I talk to Lisa?"

Bethany gave a small smile. "She and her dad went to the hospital. I doubt she'll be home at a reasonable hour, and I told her that she could miss school tomorrow, but I'll have her give you a call tomorrow."

"Thanks. Good night, Mrs. Kaye."

"Good night, Brian. And thanks again."

"No Problem."

He's a nice one, Bethany thought to herself. *Too bad they're so young.* Bethany went to the kitchen to pack up some snacks to bring to the hospital for James and Lisa.

~

"Excuse me," the nurse at the nurses' station said to James. She was looking at a clipboard given to her by the paramedic. "Are you Autumn's father?"

Now that you mention it, lady, I do see her more often than her parents, James thought to himself. "No, she's a friend of my daughters. She was at my house when she collapsed. We're still trying to reach her parents."

The nurse motioned him to come to her. "Can I get you to fill out some paperwork?" she turned the papers towards James.

"Like I said, I'm not the father," James said feeling awkward.

"I know, sir," the nurse responded, "but right now, you're her guardian."

That made James feel even more awkward. As he was filling out the paperwork, a doctor came through the double doors. He put out his hand towards James. "Hi, I'm Dr. Pilkerton."

"I'm James Kaye," James responded.

"Mr. Kaye, Autumn has been through some serious trauma."

James cut in, "Dr. Pilkerton, I am not her father. Autumn is my daughter's friend. She was at my house when all this happened. My wife is trying to contact the parents."

"Well, I guess I can wait until one of them arrives. She's resting for now."

"Thank you," James said.

"Dad," Lisa began, "are you mad at Autumn?"

James put his arm around his daughter. "No, honey. I'm mad that her parents aren't here for her. Imagine if it was you, and your mom and I weren't here for you."

"I'd be scared," Lisa responded. "But you know, Autumn doesn't have the same relationship with her parents that we have. I'll bet she's more afraid of facing them now."

"That's inevitable," James told her. "Her family is about to go through a serious challenge." James gave his own words some thought. "I think it's time for your mom and me to really get to know them. They're going to need our help."

~

Bethany tried calling the Woods' home again. There was still no answer. She had already packed up the snacks for James and Lisa. Chris was finishing his homework. Bethany told him to stay put, stay off the phone, and do a lot of praying. She grabbed her keys and left for the hospital. It was 7:45 P.M.

CHAPTER 24

Within five minutes of Bethany making her phone call, Dena Woods pulled up to her driveway. She pushed the button on the garage remote and drove her car in. She pushed the button a second time, and the garage door went down. She walked in the house through the door connecting the garage and the kitchen. She never saw the large note taped to her front door. Dena was exhausted. The lights in the house were all off, so she figured if anyone was home, they must be in bed. She went in her bedroom, kicked her shoes off, got out of her work clothes, put on her night clothes, and fell on her bed to sleep.

~

James and Lisa were sitting in the waiting room. The T.V. was showing a reality show. People were being dared to eat disgusting things. As they watched, James could not help to think aloud: "People sure are stupid," he said with a head nod.

Lisa smiled in agreement. "All the kids in my classes talk about at school are these dumb shows."

A commercial came on next. It showed an animated cave man and dinosaurs.

Senator Hopkins is at it again. His prehistoric views will set this Nation back thirty years. He wants to cut taxes for the rich and cut funding to good social programs designed to help our children. He refuses to acknowledge marital status between same-sex couples that love each other. He wants to raise hostilities with our neighbors by building a ridiculously expensive fence around our borders. America can't afford to go back to the Stone Age. Vote for Governor Clayton.

"God help us if that man gets into office," James grumbled.

"Most of my teachers love him," Lisa said. "Ms. Wallace brags about him all the time."

"Why does that not surprise me?" James rhetorically asked. "Let's talk about her for a moment. Are you certain that she took Autumn for the abortion?"

"I'm pretty sure, Dad. Autumn told me that she was meeting with Ms. Wallace after school. If Autumn needed help with an abortion, I think she would have asked Ms. Wallace. I didn't know that teachers could do that."

James shook his head. When he was an assistant

principal, he saw it all. "The public school system is an interesting animal full of contradictions. You can't give a girl an aspirin without her parents' knowledge, but you can take her for an abortion. Unbelievable!" James walked over towards the T.V. and turned it off.

At that moment, Bethany came into the waiting room with snacks in hand. The clock on the wall showed 8:35. "How are you two doing?"

"We're fine," James answered.

"What's the word on Autumn?" Bethany asked.

"All we know is that she went through some trauma and she's resting," James answered. "The doctor wants to discuss it with the parents. Speaking of which, are they on their way?"

"There's still no answer. These people must work some long hours," Bethany said.

James thought about that for a second. "That used to be me. Remember?"

Bethany nodded. "I remember the nights when I thought you would be spending the night at work. There was that one anniversary night when we had nice dinner arrangements, and at the last moment, your boss said you had to stay and help get the budget done. How anyone can just turn their life over to another person to control bewilders me," she exclaimed. "Yet millions of people do it everyday, and they don't give it a second thought. How sad!" She turned to her daughter, "Lisa," Bethany asked, "Are you ready to go home?"

"I don't know," Lisa answered. "I'd kind of like to find out what's going on with Autumn first."

"I'm going to ask the nurse if they can tell us anything," Bethany said. She went over to the nurses' station. "Hi there," she addressed the nurse. "I'm Bethany Kaye. Autumn Woods is my daughter's best friend. We've been trying to reach her parents for hours. Could you tell me what her condition is?"

The nurse looked a bit annoyed. "All I can tell you is that she's resting fine. There's not much more I can tell you. Do you think her parents will arrive soon?"

"That's the question of the day," Bethany said. Bethany went back to James and Lisa who were eating. Bethany remembered to bring James some chocolate, his greatest weakness. "You were supposed to eat the apple first," she scolded him.

"But if I eat the apple last, it will clean my teeth," James said with a smile.

"That assumes you're going to eat the apple," Bethany retorted. "I'm going to try Autumn's house again." She pulled out her cell phone. The phone rang and then went dead. "That's weird," Bethany said, looking at the phone.

"What?" James asked.

"It rang once and went dead."

"Maybe this is a bad reception area," Lisa suggested.

"I'll try again." Bethany hit the redial button. The phone rang. This time there was some clatter, and then it went dead. "Now that's weird! It sounded like someone picked it up and put it back down." She hit redial again.

～

Dena Woods heard her phone ring again. "Gosh dangit!" she yelled out while reaching for the phone again. She picked it up, "Can't you get the hint!" she yelled, and she dropped the phone back down on the cradle. She glanced at her alarm; 8:52 it said.

～

"Oh, my God!" Bethany said aloud. "She's there, but she hung up." She hit redial again.

～

Once again, Dena's phone rang. Dena was ready to scream and cry. She picked it up, "What! I'm trying to sleep!" Her voice sounded like she was in agony.

"This is Bethany Kaye, Lisa's mom—"

"Your daughter's not here," Dena interrupted. "Please don't call back; I'm trying to sleep." And again, Dena hung up the phone.

～

Bethany was furious. "If I ever get to talk to this lady, she's going to need a room next to her daughter."

James and Lisa were practically laughing. They watched Bethany hit the redial button again.

~

Dena could not believe her phone was ringing again. This time she was more alert. She picked up the phone, "What, Mrs. Kaye? What do you want?" she said with a painful voice.

"Listen up, Mrs. Woods!" Bethany commanded, "I'm calling you from the hospital, and your daughter is here. We've been trying to reach you for hours. Did you bother to check your answering machine?"

"Did you say Autumn is there?" Now Dena was sitting up in her bed.

"That's correct," Bethany answered sharply. "She has been admitted, and the doctor has been waiting to talk to her parents." *And so have we!* she thought to herself.

Dena was wide awake now. "Is she okay? What's going on?"

Bethany knew she had her attention now. "Calm down. It's too long of a story for the phone. They haven't told us anything because we're not the parents. All I can tell you is that she's been through some trauma, and she's resting now."

"I'll be there as soon as I can." And she hung up the phone.

~

Bethany looked at James and Lisa. "She's on her way."

"Good," James said. "I'm dying to ask her where the heck she's been and why she doesn't check her messages."

"I think we can skip that one tonight," Bethany responded.

"Be nice, Dad," Lisa warned.

"Is her father coming too?" James asked

"I didn't get that impression," Bethany answered.

"Dad, her father is probably out of town. He's always on some business trip. I guess I should tell you," Lisa began. "Autumn's mom thinks he's cheating on her."

"And where did you get that information?" Bethany asked.

"From Autumn. That's what her mom told her, and she told me."

"That's real nice," James said sarcastically.

"What do you mean, Dad?"

"Honey," James began, "that's very private information. My guess is that Autumn trusted you enough to share it. But did it occur to you that maybe he's *not* cheating on her?"

"Dad, I didn't say I believed her. In fact, I didn't say anything."

Bethany chimed in. "Yes, Honey, but unless Autumn's mom knows that for sure, she shouldn't be saying that to her kids. It's things like that that cause families to lose trust with each other and split apart."

"Mom, I think that will probably happen anyway. Her parents are never together."

"I think they'll find some time now," James said.

At 9:38, Dena Woods walked into the emergency room of the hospital. She was wearing sweats, her hair was a mess, and her make-up was mostly worn off.

James had never really met Dena before, and Bethany had only met her a few times. Dena walked up to the Kayes. "I'm so sorry!" she said with a look of embarrassment. Her eyes began to tear. "You must think I'm—"

James cut in, "Mrs. Woods, don't worry about what we or anyone else thinks. Right now, your daughter needs you." James and Bethany briefly told her the situation with her daughter. For a moment, James thought Mrs. Woods was going to either pass out or be sick. "We'll stay here with you for now. Go see your daughter. Is her father coming?"

"He doesn't know any of this is happening. He's out of town." There was disdain in Dena's voice.

"I'm sure he'll want to know," Bethany asserted.

"I doubt it. Let me go see Autumn for now and talk to the doctor."

"I think that's a good idea," Bethany said. "I think the hospital has a stack of papers for you to fill in when you're done." Dena walked to the nurses' desk, told them who she was, and they gave her a clipboard with a stack of papers on it, and showed her to her daughter's room.

When Dena walked up to Autumn's bed, Autumn was asleep. Dena reached out and gently grabbed her daughter's hand. She began to cry, and in a whisper she said, "I'm sorry I wasn't here for you, Honey."

Autumn's eyes fluttered open. She looked up at her mother and said, "Mom, I'm sorry I did this to you. It's all my fault."

Dena reached down and half-hugged her daughter. "It's okay. I'm here. You're okay now." Dena rose back up still holding Autumn's hand. "Are you feeling okay? Are you in pain?"

"I feel better than I did," Autumn responded. "I still have pain down there though. Am I going to be okay?"

Dena paused for a moment. "I'm sure you will. I haven't spoken to the doctor yet, so I don't have all the information. Why don't you get some rest now? I'm going to talk to your friend's parents for a minute and let them get home, and then I have all this paperwork to do."

"Is Lisa still here?" Autumn asked.

Dena felt badly all over again. "Yes, she's been here with her father a long time. I feel like such a bad parent."

"You're a good mom, Mom. Does Dad know?"

Dena was hesitant, "I haven't called him yet." She went quiet and looked at her daughter's eyes that still had tears in them. "Do you want him to know?"

Autumn did not speak for a moment and started to cry even more. "No," she finally responded. "I do want him here though."

"I'll tell him then." Dena walked out of the room. She went up to the Kayes who looked exhausted. "I'm so sorry I put you through this. You look like you need to sleep. Please go home."

"We're okay," Bethany said. "We're glad we could be there for your daughter."

"I'm just glad she was with friends," Dena said. "She wants me to call her father."

"I think you should," James responded.

"I just don't know if I want him here," Dena said.

"Mrs. Woods," James addressed, "as a father, I can tell you that he would want to be with his daughter—even if you don't want him here. I also think your daughter needs both of her parents right now."

"It's funny you say that, because as much as Autumn doesn't want him to know, she does want him here. I'll call him in the morning."

"I think you should call him now," Bethany said. "In a situation like this, it shouldn't matter what time of the day it is."

"You're right," Dena said. She picked up her cell phone and punched in Curt's number.

CHAPTER 25

It was 1:47 A.M. ET when Curt's cell phone began to ring. He jumped up from his hotel bed startled. *Who would have the nerve to call me at this time,* he thought to himself. He looked at his phone and recognized Dena's number. "It's after one in the morning here," he said in a groggy voice. "This better be good."

Dena was not happy with the response. "Is your daughter being rushed to the emergency room tonight good enough for you?"

Curt sat up quickly and turned on the light. "What's going on?" he asked with genuine concern in his voice.

"Are you alone?"

Curt responded with shock at the question. "What are you talking about! Of course I'm alone. Who did you expect me to be with? Never mind. What's going on?"

"Autumn is in the hospital. I . . . she needs you here. It's serious. She's okay, but she wants you here."

"Are you going to tell me the specifics?" Curt asked.

Dena hesitated. "I'm not sure you want to hear this over the phone; but then again, it will give you time to think about what you're going to say to her when you get here."

"Will you just tell me!" Curt commanded.

"She's had an abortion, and it didn't go well," Dena spit it out fast. The phone went quiet for a few seconds.

"Did you know about this?" Curt asked.

"No," Dena responded. "Just get here."

"I'll call my boss and pack. Tell Autumn I'm on my way."

～

Dena hung up and looked up at the Kayes. "He's on his way. Why don't you three go home. I'll stay here with my daughter and get this paperwork done."

"We'll be here in the morning," Bethany said.

"Thank you," Dena said with a lump in her throat and tears in her eyes.

Bethany reached out and took Dena's hand. "Would you mind if we pray together?"

Dena shook her head indicating that she did not mind. She found that she could not speak.

Bethany held her hand, and James and Lisa put a hand on Dena's shoulders. "Lord, we just lift up the Woods family, and especially Autumn. Lord, we just pray that you'll heal Autumn's body. We also pray that you'll bring emotional healing to the Woods family. They may not even realize how much they need you now. Lord, we just pray that you will make yourself visible to them and give them strength. And, Father, show James and Lisa and me how we can help them the most. Let us all sleep well tonight. In Jesus' name we pray. Amen."

Dena was now crying hard. She reached out to Bethany and hugged her. "No one has ever prayed for me before."

"Well, then we'll have to do it again," Bethany gave her a smile.

"Please go get some sleep."

"That sounds good," James said. He took out his pen and a piece of paper and handed it to Dena. "Here's both of our cell numbers and our home line. Call if you need us, but we'll see you tomorrow anyway. I look forward to meeting your husband."

Dena's face dropped down a bit. "Besides being tired, he's going to be in for a lot."

"Don't worry," James said, "We'll be here for you."

The Kayes left the hospital and walked out to their cars. James walked Bethany to hers in the late evening. They were tired. Bethany looked up at James. "What do you think?" she asked.

"I think it will be interesting when Mr. Woods arrives on the scene—and in more ways than one."

"Their family is about to go through the fire," Bethany added.

"The school situation will be something too," James said.

"Dad," Lisa began, "what can be done with Ms. Wallace? I mean, isn't everything she did legal?"

"Most likely," James answered. "I think I'll contact a few friends of mine for them though and find out what their rights are on this," James replied. "I think your teacher may want to watch her back a bit though."

"What do you mean?" Lisa asked.

"Lisa, Mr. Woods may be a lot of things, but he's still a father like me, and that's his little girl. I can tell you, if that was you in that hospital, Ms. Wallace would need police protection."

Bethany's expression on her face showed her disapproval towards her husband's comment. "James, do you really think you should talk like that in front of your daughter?"

James did not give it a thought, "No!"

Bethany looked at Lisa, "I think it's time to go home. Lisa, get in the car," she said.

"Lisa," James put his arm around her, "I want you to give some thought to if you want to stay at a public school." He kissed her forehead and opened up the car door for her. He then led Bethany to the other side of the car.

"I'm sorry," she said as she embraced him. "I had no idea how badly this got to you. I didn't realize until just now how angry you are."

James' throat suddenly got dry. "If that was our baby . . . I'd kill that woman."

"I bet you would." Bethany could feel his body shaking. She pulled him closer, squeezed him tightly, and gave him a kiss. "I'll see you at home."

CHAPTER 26

Curt picked up his phone and dialed his boss's cell number. His hope was that his boss would not answer and that he could just leave a message. But that was not the case. "This is Frank."

"Hi, Mr. Robbins," Curt said with surprise in his voice.

"Curt?" his boss asked in surprise.

"Yes, Sir, I'm sorry to be calling you so late."

"Curt, I'm shocked you're calling me at all. It's got to be close to 2:00 there."

"Yes, Sir," Curt confirmed in a tired voice, "that sounds about right. Mr. Robbins, I just received an emergency call from home. My daughter is in the emergency room. I'm packing up to head home now."

"Is it serious? Is she okay?" Frank Robbins asked in a curious voice.

Curt caught the tone. It sounded to him like his boss was asking if it was serious enough that he *really* had to leave. "Mr. Robbins, for my wife to call me, it must be serious."

"Well, sometimes wives react over-emotionally," his boss said. "Is she in critical condition?"

Curt was beginning to burn up. He had been with his company for eleven years; he had been a great "team player," as they liked to say; and even in today's society where loyalty was not expected from either employee or employer, Curt was always the one they could count on. And now, he was being asked to choose between his company and his daughter. "Mr. Robbins, do you think I would even bother you at this time of the night if I didn't believe this was serious?"

"All I'm saying, Curt, is that this deal is very important to us, and we are counting on you to take care of it."

"Mr. Robbins, my daughter is counting on me too, and I need to be there for her. I'm sure you would understand if it was your daughter." *I can't believe I'm having to go through this,* Curt thought to himself.

"Do what you think is best, Curt," his boss responded. "I do want to remind you that you are up for a pay review next month."

Curt was ready to explode, but he knew he had to hold it back. "Yes, Sir. I'm sorry, Sir. I will get it done when I know that my daughter is okay. And I'm sorry to have disturbed you." Curt hung up the phone. He cursed aloud almost yelling. He had a sick feeling knowing that he had just basically asked for permission to go see his daughter in the hospital. He was wide awake now.

CHAPTER 27

Early in the morning the Kaye's phone rang. Bethany answered it.

"Hi, Bethany. It's Linda. Brian told me that you were at the hospital last night with Lisa's friend. How is she?"

Bethany was awake but tired. "Hi, Linda. Her friend has really gone through a lot. I can't get into it now."

Linda knew enough not to pry. "What can I get out on the prayer chain?"

"Let them know that this girl needs physical and emotional healing, and that this family needs the Lord," Bethany answered. "We're going to see them this morning. Could you tell Brian—or should I say, my future son-in-law—to pick up Lisa's assignments."

Linda laughed at the comment. "Will do. Just for the record; my son has good taste in women."

"James and I were saying the same thing. We're not ready to see Lisa date yet, although we can't stop her from noticing guys. With all these freaky kids out there, we're just glad that she noticed Brian. We told her that he comes from a good family."

"Thank you," Linda said. "We feel the exact same way. Will you give me a call when you get back?"

"Sure thing," Bethany answered. "I'll call you back."

Bethany got off the phone and began making breakfast. James' appointments were not until later. The plan was that Chris would still go to school, but James, Bethany, and Lisa would go to the hospital.

Bethany remembered that she needed to call the school to let them know that Lisa would not be there today. A staff member answered and Bethany told her that Lisa had a friend in the hospital and would be there for most of the day.

"Mrs. Kaye," the woman responded, "that is not a legitimate excuse for being absent."

This annoyed Bethany, "Who says?"

"The State of California, Mrs. Kaye. It's in the Ed. Code."

Bethany had no tolerance for this. "Bummer! Oh, well, I guess you better let the governor know too then. Lisa still will not be there today. Thank you." And Bethany put down the phone. *We've got to get our kids out of the public schools,* she thought to herself.

The attendance officer at the school let Kim Faretti know about the conversation with Lisa Kaye's mother. Kim picked up the phone and called the Kaye house.

Bethany was about to leave the kitchen when the phone rang again. "Hello," she answered.

"Hello, Mrs. Kaye. This is Mrs. Faretti, the assistant principal at Lisa's school."

"Hello, Mrs. Faretti. What can I do for you?" Bethany said with a frustrate tone.

"Mrs. Kaye, I was told that Lisa is going to miss school today because she's going to visit a friend in the hospital. Is that correct?"

"That is correct. We're just getting ready to leave now," Bethany replied.

"Mrs. Kaye, I'm sure this is important to Lisa, but the compulsory education laws of California state that the only excused absence from school is the actual student being sick or in the hospital."

"Mrs. Faretti," Bethany began, "I'm not trying to be rude to you, but I really don't care. My daughter is not perpetually absent from school—heck, half the time she's legitimately sick, I make her go to school anyway. But Mrs. Faretti, this is also a family matter too. We're meeting the family of this girl at the hospital to help them through this situation."

"That's really nice of you." Kim said sincerely. "Is this girl a student here?"

"Yes, she is. And I'm guessing that her parents will likely forget to call her in absent today."

"May I ask what happened to her," Kim inquired.

"Mrs. Faretti," Bethany answered, "my guess is that you will find out exactly what happened really soon, because this incident directly involves the school and one of its teachers."

That sent a chill up Kim's spine. As a school administrator, she had experienced bad situations with teachers, and those situations never went away quickly. "Could I ask you to give me more information?" Kim asked.

"Believe me, I'd love to; but I don't believe it would be right for me to overstep the parents that are directly involved with this," Bethany said. "I will tell you this: My husband and I are extremely concerned about this as well. You have some renegade teachers with extreme political agendas there, and at least one, in particular, has no problem shoving it down the students' throats. My husband and I are seriously considering pulling our daughter out of the public school system.

"I'm not trying to sound like a fanatic or even build up unnecessary drama, but I'm very serious when I tell you that when this girl gets out of the hospital, the very next thing her parents will do is beat down the door of this school, and it's going to be ugly."

Kim decided that the best thing to do was to get off of the phone. "Mrs. Kaye, I appreciate you frontloading me about this. I need to let you know before we hang up that you will be receiving a letter from the school regarding the un-excused absence. What you do with it is up to you."

"That's fine," Bethany said.

"I also want you to know that I care about these students. Please let that little girl know that she's in my pray . . . thoughts."

"I'll do that. Thank you."

Kim walked out of her office and into Carl Lane's office. She told him about the conversation she had just had with Bethany Kaye.

"It's funny how the Kayes' name has been popping-up a lot lately," Carl said. "Any idea on who the girl in the hospital might be?"

"No, but I do know the students Lisa hangs around. I'll ask a few of them what they know discretely."

"Yeah, keep it discrete," Carl echoed. "What do you think? Is Mrs. Kaye trying to make a mountain out of a molehill?"

Kim thought for a second, "I don't think so. There are too many things that tell me she should be taken seriously. This girl being in the hospital is one of them."

"I guess we'll find out soon enough," Carl said.

And the train rolls on, Kim thought to herself.

CHAPTER 28

At 8:17 a.m. Curt finally arrived at the hospital. He had not slept much on the plane. And how could he? How does any father sleep knowing that his fourteen-year-old daughter has had sex and an abortion, and because of that, is now in the hospital. His mind was racing: *How could this have happened? Why would she do this? She knows better. What do I say to her? Is Summer having sex too? Why would Dena think I was cheating on her? I work like a slave trying to provide for my family, and that's the thanks I get? Why is this happening? Doesn't God have better things to do then pick on me?*

He walked into the emergency room and saw Dena sitting on a chair asleep. Her hair was a mess, and she had no make-up on. Curt tapped her shoulder, and she awoke. "I made it," was all he could think to say at first. "Can I go see her?"

"It's not visiting hours yet," Dena answered, as she looked at her watch.

"Did you spend the night here?" Curt asked.

"Yes," Dena said a little annoyed. "I thought that would be obvious to you."

Curt tried to make up for his question, "Well, if it's any consolation, I didn't sleep on the plane ride here. All I could think about was what I was coming to. Is she okay?"

"That's what I'm waiting to find out. They did some tests and examinations last night, and I think this morning too. I'm pretty sure she's resting now."

Curt walked over to the nurse's station. He saw the graveyard-shift nurse. "I'm Autumn Woods' father," he announced. "When will the doctor be able to give us some information?"

"The doctor will be in sometime after 8:30," she answered.

"That could be anytime," Curt said with annoyance.

"Yep. Doctors are unpredictable."

"Is there any information *you* can give me?" Curt asked.

"I'm sorry, sir. I can't. She's had a few tests, and she's resting well"

Curt walked back over to Dena. "She can't tell me anything."

"I could have told you that," Dena said back coldly.

"Don't you think I would have told you if I knew something?"

Curt gave that some thought. "You know, sometimes it's the subtle hints you give that help you to really communicate. Tell me something: Do you think I'm cheating on you?"

"I will not discuss this here or now," Dena said defensively. She got up and started to walk away. "I'm going to the lady's room and try to look human again."

Curt briefly followed her. "That is what you think. I have *never* cheated on you."

Dena turned quickly and faced him. "I said I don't want to talk about this here." Dena turned away and went inside the restroom.

At that moment James, Bethany, and Lisa Kaye walked in the waiting room. They walked right by Curt not recognizing him. Bethany walked up to the nurse and asked about Autumn.

Curt heard his daughter's name mentioned and approached the Kayes. "Hi there. I heard you ask about my daughter." He looked at Lisa, "Oh, Lisa, I'm sorry. I didn't recognize you. I haven't seen you in a long time. How did you know she was here?"

Lisa looked at Curt strangely. Thankfully, her father cut in. "We're the ones that called the ambulance. She was having dinner at our house yesterday."

Now it was Curt feeling strange. He looked down towards his feet. "Thank you for being there for her," he said in a humble voice. Curt was feeling shame. *This man and his family were the only ones there for my daughter,* he thought to himself. *I'm a lousy father!*

James put his hand out, "I'm James Kaye. You know my daughter, Lisa, and this is my wife, Bethany."

"It's nice to formally meet you. I'm a little embarrassed. Our daughters have known each other for years, but I've never really met you."

Bethany cut in, "Well, you're never home when we come by to either drop off or pick up. Autumn says that you work a lot."

"Yeah, I do," Curt replied, still feeling embarrassed. "Got to feed the family," he said trying to justify himself.

"You got to *see* the family too," James remarked.

Bethany gave James a quick tap of the toe with hers after he said that. Curt's face showed shame from the comment. James gave her a glance that indicated that he got the message.

"Can I get you some coffee, Curt?" James asked.

"Geez, after all you've done for my daughter, I think I should be the one offering you the coffee."

James put up his hand, "Curt, we're glad we could be there for her. I'll be right back with the coffee."

As James walked off, Bethany asked Curt where Dena was.

"She just stopped at the rest room. I'm sure she'll be out in a minute." Curt hesitated for a moment. He put his hands to his face, and as he removed them, he had tears in his eyes. "How did this all happen?" he asked to no one in particular.

James was already coming back with the coffee, and Dena was now walking towards them. Bethany put her hand on Curt's shoulder and suggested that he sit down.

Dena came up to the Kayes, "Hi. It's good to see you again. I see you've met Curt."

James handed Curt the coffee, and Curt said thank you in a whisper. Bethany spoke up finally, "I think this is just now hitting him."

Curt gave a nod.

"Why don't you two go in and see your daughter for a few moments," James suggested. "I think she'd like to know that her father is here for her."

Curt got back to his feet. "I want to go see her."

Curt and Dena went into Autumn's room. She was awake and the T.V. was on, but Autumn looked like she was staring right through it. She saw movement out of the corner of her eye and turned to see her parents. Then, she turned away.

Dena came to the bed and grabbed her hand. Curt put his hand on her forehead and stroked her hair. "How are you feeling?" Dena asked.

"I'm tired," Autumn responded in almost a whisper.

"Autumn," Curt began, "I'm sorry I wasn't there for you, but I'm here now. Do you want to talk about it?"

Autumn began to cry. She nodded her head no.

"Alright, honey," Dena acknowledged, "we'll talk when you're ready."

At that moment, the doctor walked in. He was tall and young looking. "Hi, are you Autumn's parents?"

Curt held out his hand, "I'm Curt Woods, her father, and this is my wife, Dena."

"I'm Dr. Pilkerton, Mr. Woods," he said shaking Curt's hand. "Your daughter's been through a lot. Let's go down the hall for a moment." He led them to a small office area down the hallway. "Mr. and Mrs. Woods, Autumn went through some serious trauma for a girl her age."

"Was this some kind of botched abortion?" Curt asked.

"Believe it or not, no," the doctor answered. "I don't do these things, but the fact of the matter is that your daughter's body did not respond or recover well from it. Do you know where she got it done?"

Curt and Dena looked ashamed. They were still working on that one. "Dr. Pilkerton," Dena began, "we don't know what happened yet. We just now tried to talk to her about it, but she didn't want to talk. We just don't know."

Curt cut in with a slight angry tone. "Dr. Pilkerton, I'm not sure I get this. Do doctors make a habit of performing medical procedures on minors without their parent's permission?"

"Mr. Woods, as I said, I don't do these things, but

the fact is, the law states that a minor can get an abortion without her parents' permission. There are health clinics all over the place. Planned Parenthood makes it easy for young ladies to do it."

"But you don't just drop in to one of these places and walk right back out," Dena countered.

"No, that's true," Dr. Pilkerton affirmed. "You'll have to find that out from your daughter."

"What's the bottom line, Doctor?" Curt asked. "Is she going to be okay?"

"She will slowly recover with some pain," the doctor explained. "But, I fear that she may have a significant challenge in the future when she really does want to have a child."

"Are you saying she can't have kids?" Dena asked, now with tears in her eyes.

The doctor's face looked doubtful, "I can't say for sure. I very much doubt it. She suffered a lot of trauma down there. But God proves doctors wrong all the time. In the meantime, it looks like the bleeding has stopped, but I want to keep her here one more night for observation. If I may suggest something?" The Woods gestured approval. "Don't push too hard on trying to get the story out of her. First of all, I don't want her feeling any more stress than what she already does, and I want her to sleep. My guess is, when she's ready, she'll tell you everything. I'll be back to check on her later tonight—unless I need to come back sooner; which the nurses would let me know—and then once more in the morning before she's discharged." He reached in his pocket and handed a card to Dena. "Here's my card if you have any questions that can't wait. My guess is that I'll see you later anyway, but you two need to get some rest too."

"Thank you, Doctor," they both said.

They went back to Autumn's room. Her eyes were shut, but it was obvious she was awake. Autumn did not open her eyes, but she knew her parents were back in the room. "What did the doctor say?"

"He said you're going to be okay, and you'll probably go home tomorrow," Dena answered.

"He probably thinks I'm a little slut," Autumn said.

"No," Curt said, "I think he just wants you to get better. Autumn, your mom and I aren't mad at you. We want you to get better. We *would* like to talk about all this, but we can wait 'till you're ready."

"You'll probably have to be at a business meeting by that time," Autumn admonished him.

Curt did not like it, but he kept his cool. The fact was she had a right for feeling that way. "Actually, I'm going to be taking some time off. Your mom and I have a lot to discuss too. The fact is my family needs me for right now."

Dena did not respond to any of Curt's comments, and she decided to change the subject a bit. "Your friend Lisa is outside with her parents."

"Mom, I'd really like to talk with her . . . alone."

"Sure," Dena said, "I'll tell her to come in. In the meantime, your father and I will come back later."

Dena and Curt walked out of the room to the waiting area where the Kayes were. "Lisa, Autumn would like to see you. Do you want to spend some time with her?"

"Yeah, I'd like that," Lisa responded. Lisa went to the room.

"My wife and I would like to have lunch with you today," James said.

"Oh, I think you have done enough," Dena replied.

"To be honest with you," James began, "that wasn't really a request. Bethany and I would really like to sit and talk for awhile."

"There are some things we'd like to share with you, and we think it's time that our families got better acquainted," Bethany added.

"Well, I think it's the least we can do," Curt said. "But we're buying."

"No," said James, "This was our offer. You can get the next one. Why don't you two go take a nap for a couple hours. We'll meet you at 1:00, at the BJ's Restaurant across the street."

"That sounds good," Curt said. "They have great calzones."

A few minutes later, Lisa came back to the waiting area and told them that Autumn was tired and wanted to sleep. Both families said goodbye for the time.

CHAPTER 29

Kim Faretti was conducting her investigation. She pulled Lisa Kaye's class schedule as well as the daily absence list. She went to see Wendy Swarengen first. Wendy was teaching her English class when Kim came in the door of her classroom. Wendy saw her and gave the class a quick direction while she stepped aside to see what Kim wanted.

"Sorry to interrupt," Kim said apologetically, "I have a quick question for you. Do you know who some of Lisa Kaye's good friends are?"

Wendy had a curious look on her face. "I know that she's friends with Tammy Ramirez, Ashley Clem, another girl that I don't have in my class, and I think Brian Holm. I saw that she's on the absence list. Is she okay?"

"Oh, she's fine. Thanks. I appreciate it," Kim said. She walked out quietly and then checked her absence list.

All of the names she was given were not on the list. Those students were currently on campus.

She then went into Stan Norburg's room. She asked the same question to him.

"I don't pay much attention to those things, but I'm pretty sure she's good friends with Autumn Woods and Tammy Ramirez. Is Lisa in trouble?"

"No, not at all," Kim said.

"She's such a good kid," Mr. Norburg said. "Unfortunately, I'm going to be giving her her first F."

That caught Kim's attention. "Really? What was the assignment?"

"I gave the kids a sort-of research/biography on a historical figure. She chose one that can't be proven really even existed."

"Who did she choose?" Kim asked with curiosity.

"Jesus," Mr. Norburg responded. "Technically, he's a myth or legend; besides, this is a history class not a world religion class. The paper itself was pretty-well written though."

Kim got that sick feeling again. She could just picture the scene of Mr. and Mrs. Kaye coming to the school about this one. But Stan Norburg was in the middle of teaching his class, and this was no time to talk about it. "Stan, do me a favor and pop by my office during your prep time. I have something else I want to run by you."

"Sure," Mr. Norburg said. Kim walked out. *Crap! Here we go again,* Kim thought to herself. She had almost forgotten to look at the absence list in her hand. When she did, she saw the name Autumn Woods and the letters NC next to the name which meant No Call. Kim went to a couple more of Lisa's teachers, and the same names kept coming up. She then went back to her office, pulled up Autumn's personal information, and called her house. No answer. *Well, there's only one way to find out,* Kim thought. She pulled out the phone book and looked up the closest hospital to Autumn's address. The lady on the other end answered. "Hi, I'm trying to find out if Autumn Woods is a patient there." The nurse asked her to wait a moment; then she came back on. "Oh, she is. Thank you so much." Kim hung up the phone and went to Carl Lane's office to let him know.

CHAPTER 30

"What do you plan on saying to them," Bethany asked James.

"I think I want to just get to know them first. I think they already know they need help. Let's get them to open up and see just how much they need."

James pulled into the BJ's Restaurant parking lot and found a spot. They decided earlier to leave Lisa home to get caught up on her school assignments. The restaurant was busy and a little noisy with big-screen TV's and sports on all of them. James knew that the atmosphere was just okay, but the food was very good. They looked around the restaurant to see if the Woods were there yet. They were not, so James and Bethany had the hostess seat them at a table for four. The waiter came over to them quickly. They told the waiter, Steve his name tag said, that they were waiting for another couple. The waiter was very polite and said that he would watch for them.

The waiter brought some water and asked if they would like to order some drinks while they were waiting. James ordered a Dr. Pepper and Bethany ordered a strawberry lemonade. The waiter left four menus and said he would be right back. James saw the door open and Curt and Dena walked through. James waved his hand so they could see him, and Curt waved back and headed towards the table.

Steve came to the table with the drinks and saw that the other party had arrived. He asked if he could bring them drinks as well. A Coke and Sprite were ordered. Steve handed them menus and said he would be back in five minutes to take their order. James asked Steve how old he was.

"I'm twenty-three, sir." He responded.

"You seem to be a very sharp young man. Are you going to college?"

"I graduated last year," Steve responded.

"What are you doing here?" James asked.

Steve's face took on a look of shame. "I guess college degrees aren't paying off like they used to. In the meantime, I have to work. I've got student loans"

"What was your major?" James asked.

"Business. But the job market is really bad, and nothing is paying enough for me to be able to move out." He decided to change the subject. "I'll be right back with the other drinks and to take your order."

Bethany looked at James, "What do you think?"

"We'll watch and wait," he answered. Then he looked over at Curt and Dena, "Glad you could join us. Were you two able to get a little rest?"

"Not really," said Curt.

Dena spoke up, "We mostly stayed with Autumn. She's scared and an emotional basket case right now."

"I bet," said Bethany. "My guess is she's not the only one."

That brought a moment of silence. Finally, Curt spoke up, "We're just trying to figure out how all this happened and where to go from here. What do you guys think?"

Steve came back at that moment. "Hi folks, I'm sorry that took longer than I expected. We had a bit of a mess in the back. Are you ready to order?"

"I am," said James. "I always know what I want here."

"We're still looking, but by the time you take their orders, we'll be ready," said Dena.

"What do you like here?" said Curt.

James looked up at Steve and said, "I will have a calzone with pepperoni and meatballs." He looked at Curt, "How's that sound?"

Curt shook his head up and down.

Bethany was next. "I'll have the calzone with pepperoni, black olives, and peppers."

Steve looked over at Curt and Dena. Curt made his decision, "I'll have a calzone with sausage and mushrooms."

"And you, ma'am?" Steve asked.

"I think I'll have the pasta salad," Dena said.

"Rebel," James joked.

"Thank you, folks. I'll get that in right now and be back to fill your drinks," Steve said and walked off.

"So far he's good," Bethany said to James.

"What's that all about?" asked Curt.

"James recruits and develops people in his business, and he's always looking for good people," Bethany answered.

"I'll talk to him later," James said, "but I think the question on the table was, 'What happened, and where do you go from here.'"

Curt had a look of disgust on his face. "I feel sick to my stomach."

"Not what I wanted to hear at my favorite restaurant," James remarked.

"Where did we go wrong?" Curt asked.

"We're too busy," Dena answered. "You're never home. You always have a trip to go on or a meeting to attend."

Curt got a bit defensive. "It's my job. I have to take care of the family."

"And how is that working for you, Curt?" James asked pointedly.

"So this is all my fault?" Curt protested.

Bethany was a little more subtle, "I'm sure that when this whole situation gets analyzed, there will be plenty of blame to go around. What you two really need to do is take a look at the whole picture of your family. What do you know that you're doing right; and what do you think needs to change?"

Before either of them could answer, James cut back in. "For instance, your marriage. Bethany and I have already picked up that there is some serious tension there. Are you two holding together?"

"Well—" Curt started.

"No!" Dena cut him off emphatically. "It's not good. He's never home. He spends more time with his secretary than his family."

Curt got angry quickly. "Are you suggesting that I'm cheating on you with my secretary?"

Dena stayed quiet.

"I'll have you know," Curt began, "that even though I spend the night at the office, she clocks out at 5:00 sharp and goes home to her husband." Curt was burning up at the accusation. "It's bad enough these people think I'm a bad father; I'm not going to sit here and allow you to make them think I'm some scum-bag husband! I work my tail off for my family!"

James knew he had to put out the fire quickly. "Let's everyone calm down. Curt, we don't believe either of you are bad parents or bad spouses. We do believe that you two need some help from people who care about you."

Bethany jumped back in. "Look, the fact is that most of us don't get Parenting 101 class or How to Run a Family Basics. Typically, people wing it and go day-by-day—we figure it out as we go. James and I aren't the perfect parents. We've screwed up many times."

"Your daughter isn't in the hospital from a bad abortion right now though," Curt shot out in frustration.

"No, she isn't," said James. "Bethany and I took a lot of time in instilling values into our kids, but there're still no guarantees. We're doing everything we can to show them what God wants for their lives."

"How can you know?" Dena asked. "Seriously, how can you know what God wants for them?"

Steve arrived with the food and began distributing the plates to their rightful owners.

"Steve," James began, "I'm looking for some quality people to develop in my business. Are you keeping your options open?"

"Yes I am," Steve said with a smile. "What do you do?"

"I train and develop people to own their own business, through helping families get debt and financially-free. Wouldn't you agree there's a huge market for that right now?"

"Yep."

"Is there a good number and a time to contact you?"

Steve pulled out a piece of paper and wrote the information down. He handed it to James and said thank you.

"I'll be calling you," James told him and shook his

hand. He turned to the others, "Let me bless the meal real quickly." James said a quick prayer.

Bethany got the conversation back on track. "You asked, how do we know what God wants for our children. The Bible says in Micah 6:8, 'He has told you, oh man, what the Lord requires of you. To do justly, love mercy and walk humbly with your God.'"

"Oh, come on!" Curt grumbled. "The Bible doesn't teach kids about abortion and the things that are going on in today's world. And besides, everyone knows that the Bible is subject to interpretation and full of mistakes."

"Really?" James responded with sarcasm. "And how many times have you read it all the way through in your lifetime?"

"Look, I'm not saying the Bible isn't a good book. I'm—"

James cut Curt off, "You still haven't answered my question. How many times have you read the Bible all the way through?"

Curt looked like a child with his hand caught in a cookie jar. "Never."

"Okay," James started again, "How many times have you actually opened the Bible?"

Curt again looked sheepish. "Never. But I do know a lot of things the Bible says," he tried to recover.

"Such as?" James asked with a smile on his face.

Curt thought for a moment. "'God helps those who help themselves; Money is the root of all evil; Thou shall not kill; Do good to your fellow man,'" Curt had a smile on his face now.

James' smile was bigger. "Congratulations! You got one out of four." The ladies were laughing now as well.

Curt was getting frustrated now. "You're telling me that those words aren't in the Bible?"

"No," James responded, "I'm telling you that three out of the four aren't in the Bible. 'Thou shall not kill' is one of the Ten Commandments."

Dena chimed in, "I don't mean to be rude, but how does this tie into our situation?"

"That's a great question," said Bethany. "Have you ever felt like you were being attacked by something you couldn't see and in many areas of your life?"

"Yes," Dena answered.

"That's because you are," said Bethany. "Everything you two and your family are going through is spiritual. You *are* being attacked."

"I want to go back to a statement you made a minute ago, Curt," James said. "You seem to be under the impression that the Bible, because it was written two-thousand years ago, has no relevance today. What if I could show you that it applies to our lives just as much today as it did back then? That, in fact, the Bible *does* teach about abortion, pre-marital sex, drugs and alcohol, and many, if not *all,* of the things that are going on today."

"That would be interesting to see," Curt responded.

"I was hoping you'd say that," James said with a smile.

"Bethany and I can prove to you that what's going on with your family is a spiritual matter."

"Would you two be willing to get together again tomorrow and talk more?"

"I guess," Dena said a little reluctantly. Curt did not respond.

"Good," Bethany responded.

The two couples began talking about what they do for a living. Curt shared that his boss was making him choose between his job and his family. Dena did not realize that Curt had been put in such a tough position.

"How long have you been working for your company?" James asked.

"Eleven years," said Curt. "You would think after eleven years they would treat you with a little dignity and care about your family."

"No, I wouldn't think that," James said. "I used to think that way years ago, but I learned that J*O*B really stands for Just Over Broke. I used to let another person tell me when I could be with my family; when I could have a day off; how much money I could make; whether or not I could be at my kids' games and events, but those days are long gone. No one has that noose around my neck anymore, and they never will."

"James, I'm forty years old now; I'm too old to make a major career move. There's too much risk involved," Curt explained

"Curt," Bethany began, "risk is part of life. Better

you risk losing your job than losing your family." That produced a moment of silence. "James and I made our decision together. James was having health issues from stress, getting migraine headaches, constantly having to tell us that he couldn't make it somewhere, and having to say no all the time, because we never had enough money. Does that sound familiar?"

Curt did not get the chance to answer. "That's our lives," Dena said. "We've been living like that forever. The money is okay, but we're never together to enjoy it"

"Curt," James asked, "do you think you have a good job?"

Curt thought for a brief moment, "Well, they pay me well. I'm doing slightly below six figures, and the benefits are good too."

Dena jumped in, "He's never home, he's always stressed out, and the girls never see him—I've gotten used to not seeing him," she added with the force of a hammer.

Curt began to turn red and slammed his hand on the table. "I told you there is nothing going on! Period! End of story! I am not having an affair with my secretary!"

"This is not the time or place!" Dena cut in.

"Why not, we've told them everything else so far," Curt said with sarcasm. "You think that because every time you call, and my secretary answers because I'm always in a meeting, that I must be cheating on you. My secretary is a happily married woman with a child—not mine—on the way. She'll probably quit soon.

"So let me ask you again, Curt," said James. "Do you have a good job?"

Curt dropped his chin. When he looked back up, he had tears in his eyes. "No. Dena's right about everything else. I don't know my own family, and it's all caught up with me now. I'm completely trapped."

Very slowly, Dena grabbed his hand. "I'm sorry," she whispered.

"For what? I've done this to myself and my family."

"What if we could show you a way out?" Bethany asked. "Would you be interested?"

"Yeah, I'd take a look," Curt said with an exhausted look on his face.

The couples spoke more and got to know each other. They seemed to clique well and open up. James insisted on taking care of the bill, and they arranged to meet again the next day. The Woods went back to the hospital to see Autumn and get the latest update from the doctor.

~

James and Bethany began driving home. "I want to help them," Bethany said.

"I think we already did, but they need a lot of help in a lot of areas," James responded.

"They have a lot of areas to deal with: their daughter, their marriage, his job, the school."

"The school situation will be fun. I think we need to take some serious action on that. That health teacher took that little girl for an abortion without her parent's knowledge. If it was Lisa, you'd be bailing me out of jail," James said.

"No, I'd be in the cell next to you. We've got to help them handle this right, or that may very well happen with Curt. I think when he gets his attention turned in that direction, he could really lose it," Bethany surmised.

"Yep."

About two hours after arriving at their home, James' cell phone rang. "Hello," James answered.

"Hi, James, it's Curt."

"Hey, everything okay?"

"We're still here with Autumn. We wanted you guys to know that Autumn gets to go home tomorrow. The doctor said she's going to be okay to leave."

"That's great!" James exclaimed, but he sensed something else in Curt's voice. "Is there something else?"

Curt was slow to respond. "The doctor said that it's not likely she'll ever have children in the future." Curt sniffled.

James was soothing. "Curt, doctors are wrong frequently. They aren't God. With God, all things are possible. God loves to humble doctors. Right now, let's just celebrate that she's going to be okay and come home."

"James, you and Bethany have been the best friends we've had in ages," Curt said crying. "Dena and I need friends that care about us. We know a lot of people, but we don't have many close friends. Thank you."

"Curt, Bethany and I *want* to be there for you guys. There are many things that still need to be discussed, and we want to help you get through them."

"Thanks, James. We'll talk tomorrow."

"Get some sleep," James encouraged him. "My family will pray for all of you tonight."

"I'd like that," Curt acknowledged.

CHAPTER 31

Kim Faretti was in her office doing her number one job, discipline. Another fight had broken out between two boys. The fact of the matter was it really was not two boys; it was the two boys and the one hundred plus students that formed the circle around them to make it almost impossible to break them apart. It was like a scene out of *Animal Planet*. Between the boys fighting and the girls gossiping, it kept Kim busy.

There was a light knock at Kim's office door which was already open. Kim looked up, "Oh, come on in, Stan," she invited.

"What's up? You said you wanted to run something by me."

"Have a seat," Kim pointed to the chair as she got up to close the door.

"Uh, uh," Stan said with a smile, "she's closing the door; I'm in trouble."

Kim smiled a bit, "No, but this is important, and I'd like to try to defuse a potential bomb before it goes off."

That got Stan a little more serious. "What's this about?"

"Well, first of all, I've had a long day. There's a lot of crazy and serious stuff going on, and it seems like I'm constantly putting out the fires. After awhile, it gets old quickly, so I'm trying to prevent the fires before they start." She paused for a moment. "That said, you mentioned that you gave your students a history paper to write, and you mentioned that Lisa Kaye did hers on Jesus, and that you had to give her an F."

Stan nodded, "That's right. I hated doing it, because she's such a good kid, and the paper was well written; but Jesus is not an historical figure."

"I'm playing devil's advocate when I ask this. According to whom?" Kim asked.

"I'm not sure I understand the question," Mr. Norburg responded.

"You're saying that Jesus is not a historical figure. I'm asking, says who?"

"Oh, I see. Well, Jesus is part of the Bible and the Christian religion, but there's no evidence he ever existed," Stan explained.

"Now wait a minute," Kim began. "I'm no historian, but I've read there are other accounts of Jesus' existence outside of the Bible. They even have specials on the History Channel"

"Well, yeah, but nothing that can be substantiated," Stan defended himself.

"Well, it's my understanding that his existence can be substantiated; it's his claim to be God or the Messiah that is up for debate."

Mr. Norburg gave Kim a curious look. "Where are you going with all this, Kim?"

"Look Stan, I understand we're supposed to keep religion out of the public schools and all that—"

Stan cut in, "It doesn't sound like you agree with that."

"That doesn't matter, and it's not the point," Kim responded. "The point is, are you ready to totally and completely defend your stance and the grade you're giving Lisa?"

Stan still looked confused. "I guess so. I still don't see where you're going with this, Kim."

"Stan, I'm going to make you a guarantee as to what's going to happen when Lisa comes home with her F. I'm going to get a phone call from her parents, who are *very* sharp people, may I add, and they're going to want to talk about this. Now, I will defer them to the teacher first, because that is the respectful and professional thing to do. I also know that you will likely stand your ground. After that, they will want to meet again with me included. And, I have gotten to know this family as of late. They will come with every historical book and web site—and the Bible—to defend their daughter's choice of historical figures to write about. And at that point, you will have to defend your grade in front of me. And if you are going to give them the same reasons you just gave me, I won't be able to take your side. I can't make you change your grade, but I really think you should reconsider this."

Stan got defensive. "Why? I'm right. Regardless of what the Bible or some historians say, there's no concrete evidence that Jesus existed."

"Are you absolutely, one-hundred percent sure of that?" Kim stared hard at him.

Stan stuttered a bit. "Heck, how can anyone be one-hundred percent sure about someone who supposedly existed two-thousand years ago?"

Kim decided to take a different approach. "Isn't it true that there's no evidence that Shakespeare existed?"

"Well, there are those that say it was Marlow, but most people believe Shakespeare lived and wrote all the plays and poems."

"What about Abe Lincoln? Isn't it true that no one knows exactly where his remains are?"

Stan got a bit frustrated. "Oh, come on, Kim. We all know Lincoln existed."

"Stan, our history line is dated BC and AD, Before Christ and After Death. Now I know that those initials have been changed to make things politically correct, but originally, that's what they stood for. We have a whole curriculum that teaches on Islam and Muhammad; in fact, we teach it as *fact*. You and I both know that there is even less evidence of his existence."

"So what are you saying," Stan asked, "I shouldn't give her an F?"

"That's your call. I think you need to think this through, including the real reason why you're giving the F," Kim suggested.

"Wait a minute," Stan got a little angry. "Are you trying to say I have some agenda or vendetta against this girl?"

Kim smiled, "I think you like Lisa. You said it yourself; she's a good kid. I do think you may have a certain disposition about Jesus and Christianity, and I think that will come out when you meet with her parents."

Stan unfolded his arms. "What would you do?"

"Well, let me ask you this. You said the paper was well written. Was it well researched too—I mean, were there other sources besides the Bible?"

Stan gave a confirming grin. "Yeah, she had a lot of different sources that she quoted from. I was kind of surprised."

"Then commend her for her research. You don't have to agree with it. But if you think it was well researched and written, grade her on that. You might even write her a note saying you don't necessarily agree with her sources, but that her paper was good. Then suggest she joins Mrs. Swarengen's debate team," she suggested with a smile.

That made Stan smile too. "I see your point." Mr.

Norburg thought for a moment. "I'm glad I don't have your job."

I'm not sure I want it anymore, Kim thought to herself. "It's not always easy. There are a lot of fires to put out everyday."

"Well, you do it well." Stan held out his hand as he stood up. "Thank you."

"Thank you for the complement," Kim reached out for his hand and shook it.

CHAPTER 32

James was in his home office making a call to a lawyer friend of his. He told his friend the situation with the Woods. After about a half-hour conversation, he put down the phone and went in the kitchen to speak with Bethany.

"Well, it doesn't look good," he told her. "Technically, everyone is within the law."

"No matter how it all went down," Bethany said disdainfully. "So everyone's butts are covered? Except, there is a girl in the hospital, in pain, who may never have kids again; and her parents, who were intentionally kept in the dark about everything from everybody, trying to find answers. Did I get it all?"

James felt the same way Bethany did. "Yeah, you got it all."

"James, we need to talk with them right away. If they

go storming into that school for that teacher's head, it could be serious."

James felt the sense of urgency. He went over to the phone to call Curt. "Hey, Curt, did I catch you sleeping yet?"

"We've just left the hospital, and we're going home," Curt answered.

"Listen, Bethany and I are looking at ways to help you two through this as much as possible. We want you here for dinner tomorrow night. Bethany will cook up something for Lisa to bring over to Autumn and Summer, and after Lisa's done with her homework, we'll drop her off, and they can spend some time together. We want to have some time with just you two."

Curt was taken aback, "James, you guys are doing too much. We can manage the kids."

"Curt, let us be your neighbors for awhile," James suggested. "We know you'll return the favor another time."

"Okay, as long as we get the chance to return the favor," Curt agreed.

"I'm easy to talk into calzones and chocolate," James jested. Bethany gave him a slap on the arm.

"What time should we be there?" Curt asked.

"I'll drop Lisa off around 6:00. We'll plan for a 6:30 dinner.

"Sounds good. See you tomorrow then."

When Curt and Dena got home, Summer was sitting on the couch watching T.V. They had almost forgotten that they had another daughter. Summer was also tall with dyed black hair. Curt went to the T.V. and shut it off.

"Hey!" Summer protested, "What was that for?"

"We have a lot of talking to do as a family," Curt answered.

"Family? What family?" Summer responded with sarcasm. "You mean there's actually a family that lives in this house?"

Curt would not be bated. "Today, and from now on, there is."

Dena had not entered the family room area yet. She was taking the sign off of the front door. But the door was open enough for her to hear the conversation.

"I think you might want to run your family idea by Mom when she comes home," Summer shot back. "By the way, what are you doing home? I thought you had another *business trip* with your secretary. Won't Mom be surprised to see you."

Dena walked into the family area to Summer's surprise. "Mom is here!" she said with authority. "And today, and from now on, a *family* lives here."

Summer was so taken off guard, all she could mumble was, "What's going on?"

"Do you know where your sister is?" Dena asked.

"No, she's probably with her friends or her boyfriend," Summer answered. "We don't really keep in touch with each others' schedules." Summer finally took a close look at her parents. "Why do you two look like you haven't slept in days?"

Curt and Dena sat down with Summer and began bringing her up to date about her sister. Dena asked if she had seen the sign on the door, but Summer said that she came in the house through the back door. Dena cleared up the whole secretary issue, and Curt made many apologies for not being there for his daughters. There was much more they wanted to say to her, and many questions they wanted to ask, but they were so exhausted, that they could not continue.

"The bottom line is that things are going to change with this family," Curt told her. But the vacant expression on his daughter's face told him that she was not taking him seriously.

Dena saw it too. "Summer, your dad and I are dead serious about changing the dynamics of this family. When your sister is back and recovered, we're going to meet together and get a lot of things straightened out. We know that there's a lot *we* don't know about, but we're not about to stand around and find out the hard way again either."

Curt and Dena told Summer what the schedule would be like for tomorrow and made it clear that she would be home after school.

CHAPTER 33

Lisa went back to school the next morning with mixed emotions. She wanted to be with Autumn when she was discharged, but she knew that she would see her later in the evening, so she would just have to wait. At the same time, she looked forward to seeing Brian again. And still, there was having to attend Ms. Wallace's class. Lisa did not want to even look at the woman.

She saw Brian before the first bell rang. He asked her how Autumn was. Lisa told him that she would be home today, but she would not give any details as to why she was in the hospital. He gave her a hug and a peck on the cheek before they went their separate ways to their classes.

When she arrived at her class, Mrs. Faretti was waiting at the doorway. She pulled Lisa aside and asked how Autumn was doing.

Lisa felt a bit awkward. "She's coming home from the hospital today," Lisa said with some reservation.

"What did the doctor have to say?" Kim probed.

Lisa's face showed how uncomfortable she felt about the questions. "I don't really know all the details," Lisa answered. "You should probably ask her parents. They will know"

"Do you think her parents will be home by this afternoon?" Kim asked.

"Probably," Lisa answered. "Can I go into my class now?"

"Sure thing." Kim watched her go in to the room. Her years of experience with teenagers told her that Lisa knew much more than she was saying, but she also knew that it was not right to push students. Besides, Kim knew the next step would be to contact Autumn's parents. She decided to wait until after lunch.

~

Later on, Lisa had received her essay back from Mr. Norburg. She was happy with the grade, but she wondered what it was specifically that he disagreed with. *Does he not think that Jesus is historical enough?* She thought to herself.

Mr. Norburg began passing out small books to the class. The books were titled, *The Islamic Perspective,* by an author whose name none of the students could pronounce. Mr. Norburg instructed the students to turn to the first chapter, and they would alternate turns reading together. Lisa felt very uncomfortable, and she looked over at her friend Tammy, who looked like she was about to explode. Tammy looked up at Lisa and nodded her head back and forth. One of the students was reading aloud, "'It is because of the Western misunderstandings of Islam that brings incorrect interpretations and biases of this peaceful and beautiful religion. Islam tolerates and respects all beliefs throughout the world. Islam believes that we are all serving the same god.'"

"Very good, Mr. Joyner," said Mr. Norburg, "Who'd like to go next?" Tammy Ramirez's hand shot in the air. "Okay, Miss Ramirez, take over."

"Well, actually, Mr. Norburg, I have a quick question."

"Sure, go ahead."

Tammy pulled out a small book of her own. It was a Quran. "Well, I decided to do some research of my own, and I have here an actual Quran. I came across this passage and many others just like it, and I'm trying to understand how it compares to this man's interpretation of Islam. It says here, 'There is no god but Allah, and Mohammad is his prophet.' And here it says, 'Then your Lord spoke to his angels and said, "I will be with you. Give strength to the believers. I will send terror into the unbelievers' hearts, cut off their heads and even the tips of their fingers.'" And this too, 'To a martyr privileges are guaranteed by Allah; forgiveness with the first gush of his blood, he will be shown his seat in paradise.' I know I'm no expert on this, but that doesn't sound peaceful, respectful, or tolerant."

The class fell uncomfortably silent. Mr. Norburg's face looked like he had just seen a naked person go by. "Miss Ramirez, I think that it's inappropriate that you would find one verse in the book—"

Tammy cut him off. "Oh, no, Mr. Norburg, I told you there are plenty more. Would you like me to read them?"

"That will be enough, Miss Ramirez!" Mr. Norburg was getting angry. "We're reading *this book* to help us understand the Muslim's point of view."

Tammy would not let up. She held up the Quran. "But this *is* their point of view. It needs no interpretation."

"Miss Ramirez, please leave my room. You are disrupting the learning environment." He went over to the intercom switch, and a voice came on. "I'm sending Miss Ramirez up to the office for continued disruption of my class. Please let one of the administrators know that she's on her way, and I will send a note with the details in a minute."

Tammy collected her books, but she still was not done. "Gee, I thought I was adding to the learning environment by reading the truth."

"Out now, Miss Ramirez! And keep your mouth shut on the way out!" Mr. Norburg was boiling. He reached into his desk for a piece of paper and began writing a note. Lisa raised her hand and said that she would bring it up for him.

Lisa took the note with her and ran up the hallway as quickly as possible to catch up to Tammy. "You certainly have no fear," Lisa told her.

"What did I do wrong?" she said confidently. "They're shoving this crap down our throats, and they want us to dress up like them too. I've had it. I'm not going to listen to this anymore without a fight. I didn't do anything wrong, and I know my parents will defend me. I told them what was happening in this class."

"What did your parents say?" Lisa asked.

"Who do you think gave me the book?"

The girls walked in the office. Lisa gave one of the ladies the note and told Tammy good luck. She realized that she had forgotten to tell her parents the details about what they were studying. She knew that her parents would feel the same way. *I'm not dressing up like a Muslim,* she said to herself.

CHAPTER 34

James was meeting with a couple that was referred to him. Their situation was bad. They got into a home they could not afford with an interest only, adjustable rate mortgage, known as an ARM. The payment had gone up, the value of the home went down, and rates went up as well—all the things that the realtor said would *not* happen. The realtor and loan company made their commissions, and the couple was now about to lose their home.

"So what do we do now?" the man asked.

"You either have to lose your house or make more money. Which one sounds better to you?" James responded.

"Make more money!" they both answered.

"Great! I can show you how to do that through my business," James explained.

"You mean do what you do?" the man asked.

"Yes. It's actually a simple business, and it pays very well."

"I don't think I'd feel comfortable doing that," the man responded.

"Well, what would be more comfortable: learning something new part-time that could put an extra $1,000 in your budget so you can stay here, or losing your home?" James asked point blank.

"I don't want to lose the home," the woman said, "but this really isn't for either of us."

"As I told you, I used to be in education before this. I didn't know it either; but I learned, and now it is second nature. I'll be happy to teach you."

The couple hemmed and hawed and gave James many "good" reasons why they could not join him. Reasons like: I don't want to work extra hours; we want to be there for the kids; family time is important to us; I have softball on Thursday nights, etc. Most of these excuses for not wanting to work were the reasons why James did what he did, so he could have the freedom he had now.

James got up from the table, handed them his card and said, "Well, I wish you all the best. Give me a call if you change your minds." And he left. He had very little patience for people who were not willing to fight for their family. This family made a big mistake, and now they were looking for some fairy godmother to zap them out of it. James dealt in reality. He wanted to help them out, but they were looking for a quick fix—which was exactly what got them into the situation they are in now. He gave Bethany a call and told her he was on his way to help her get set up for the evening activities.

~

Curt and Dena picked up Autumn from the hospital. Autumn was very quiet and still tired. They had asked her if she was ready to talk, but she declined. They figured that they should not push her yet. The doctor gave her pain pills and a note not to participate in P.E. class for at least three weeks. He told them to keep her activities at home down to a minimum as well.

When they arrived home, there was a message from the school on the machine asking them to call.

"I didn't even think to call the school today," Dena said to Curt.

"Don't worry. We can deal with it tomorrow. Besides, she has a doctor's note."

They sat down and rested for awhile before getting ready to see James and Bethany.

"The Kayes are good people," Dena said. "I wish we would have gotten to know them a long time ago."

"I wouldn't have been home long enough to get to know them. Life goes fast when you're not having fun. Heck, I can't even think of the last time I had fun."

"I want to change things right now."

"Me too."

CHAPTER 35

Kim looked up at the clock on the wall in her office. It was 6:12 p.m. She was exhausted. The days kept getting longer. She had another one of those "issues" to talk to Carl about before she left. She dreaded the conversation, because she knew where it would go. Kim often wondered why Carl had selected her to be the assistant principal. Most of the time, they did not see eye-to-eye. Their personalities were different as well. Maybe the District office felt the school needed some balance. She had reasoned a long time ago that if she was the principal, she would do things very differently. Now, she was not sure if she could see herself sticking with the education field much longer. She was physically and mentally drained.

She had interviewed Tammy Ramirez earlier to get her side of the story, and then she met with Stan Norburg. For the most part, Tammy's story and his matched. Tammy seemed to be one of those strong-willed children, and even when Stan had pulled rank on her, she still would not back down. Kim was struggling with the situation because she could see that both of them had an agenda. Stan was going to attempt to make Islam politically correct, and there was no way that Tammy was going to let him. Unfortunately for Tammy, she did cause a "disruption in the learning environment." That was the one thing that the teachers could always fall back on. Kim, once again, could not help but to be impressed with the way that Tammy supported her argument though. If it was not so controversial, it would have made for a great debate.

The interesting thing that Kim could not help to observe was the growing conflict between the teachers with heavy liberal opinions and the Christian students. These students were not backing down either. Then their parents were coming in right behind them. It was reoccurring frequently now.

Kim spent about fifteen minutes telling both sides to Carl.

"So what do you think?" Carl asked.

"I think I'm getting sick of these situations," she answered.

"Welcome to school administration," he said with a smile. "All you have to do now is make everyone happy."

Kim felt her insides getting knotted-up. The stress was getting to be too much. But something sparked inside of her, and she went on something close to a tirade. "Here's what I really think," she began. "I'm sick of the political crap that goes on here! I think that little girl defended her argument intelligently. I think she has strong convictions for a fourteen-year-old, and when they were challenged, she stood her ground well. In fact, she did a better job of defending herself than Stan did."

"That's great," Carl said with a hint of sarcasm. "All you have to do now is tell Stan that."

Kim had many thoughts going through her head. From what she had observed from the staff, they were very tolerant of Carl. Most of the staff would say Carl was "okay." But she could also tell that they did not have much respect for him. He avoided conflicts and controversies like the plague. Whatever would cause him less headaches that is what he would go with. Whether or not the problem actually got resolved, he really did not seem to care. The bottom line was he never effected change. Maybe that is how he had lasted so long in administration. Yet, he was likeable.

"Carl, we have some teachers here with some strong agendas. In my opinion, some of these agendas are inappropriate, and there are students here that seem to think the same. Some of these students are digging in too. There's a part of me that thinks there could be some incredible learning that could take place, but it seems to me that every time one of these students goes against the teacher's views, they get rank pulled on them. Then we get the blow up, and we get to deal with the parents too.

The parents are making very strong arguments like, 'Why does this teacher feel the need to shove this down my kid's throat?' The problem is, this keeps landing on *our* desks, and it's getting harder and harder to support the teacher. And to be blunt, I'm sick of it!"

Carl had to give that some thought. "In this instance, Stan was just trying to teach his students about a growing culture. What's so wrong with that?"

"Carl, he had them reading out of a very one-sided book, and next week he was going to *require* them to dress like Muslims, which I persuaded him not to. Tammy pulled out an actual Quran and read out of it; and what it said was dramatically different from what the author of this book was trying to sell. Plus, there are students with strong religious convictions in that class. If you think their parents are going to go along with this, you're crazy."

Carl looked frustrated. "These fundamentalist are getting ridiculous."

Kim did not like that. "Well, imagine the shoe on the other foot. Do you honestly think the Muslim kids would wear a yamika without a protest?"

Carl was tired too. "No, I suppose not. So the question remains, what are you going to do about it?"

Kim felt like she was just thrown under the bus. But since that was the case, she decided to take charge. "At the next staff meeting, I want *us* to address this, the political agenda stuff. I don't mind doing the talking, but I want to know that you're behind me."

"I'll be behind you, as long as you're fair about it," Carl said with reluctance.

Kim still felt like she was talking to a wimp. "Carl, with personalities like Wallace in the room, you can expect some heat. They don't seem to have any problem dishing it out. It's time they took some. But I promise to be professional."

"Okay, I'm with you."

CHAPTER 36

Before James took Lisa over to the Woods' house, she had told her parents the details about what was going on in her history class. James and Bethany were frustrated. *Here we go again,* they both thought. Bethany realized with all the recent drama in the last couple of days, she had forgotten to call Lisa's teacher and find out about her latest history lesson. They did not have much time for a proper discussion on it because the Woods were going to be arriving soon. Bethany made a mental note to give Tammy's mother a call. The good news was, they all went to church together, and so this might be a great discussion for her Wednesday night group.

The Woods arrived at the Kaye's house with two bottles of Martinelli's Sparkling Cider and a carton of chocolate chip cookie dough ice-cream. They told the Kayes that Autumn was happy to be home and even happier that Lisa was going to be with her tonight. Bethany cooked a large tri-tip roast, corn-on-the-cob, baked potatoes, and made a big salad bowl. During the dinner, James made sure he kept the conversation casual. The serious stuff demanded full attention.

After clearing the dinner dishes and ice-cream, the four adults went into the family room.

"Well," James began, "I guess it's time to talk serious. Bethany and I have some information for you that you're probably not going to be happy about." The room seemed to go dead silent. "Based upon some conversation with Lisa, we're pretty certain that one of the teachers from the school took Autumn for the abortion, which makes sense, because she would have had to have an adult with her."

"Oh, my god!" Dena said in shock.

Curt rose up, "I'll sue the school and kill the teacher!"

"Well, unfortunately you can only do one of the above, and I don't recommend you do it for the sake of your family," James said. "I spoke to a lawyer friend of mine, and he confirmed with me, that the law says that an under-age girl can get an abortion without her parent's knowledge, as long as there's an adult with her. So, like it or not, the teacher was within her rights."

"Her rights!" Curt came unglued. "And what about the parents rights? You know, the people who raised and took care of the girl all her life! What about their rights to know? And who the hell is this teacher?" Curt yelled the question.

"We're not sure, but we have a really good idea," Bethany answered in a soft voice to hopefully get Curt to settle down. "I think it would be best for Autumn to answer that question to be certain."

The room went quiet for a moment. Finally, Curt asked the big question towards Dena: "You know, I just want to know why Autumn didn't come to us?"

"That's easy," Dena responded quickly, "We're never there."

That stung Curt. "I wish I could say that that wasn't true. I need to get out of my job. James, you told me you could show me something different."

"I can," James confirmed. "But I warn you, it won't be easy, but it will be worth it. There are three major things we need to cover tonight, and all are going to take time, patients, and effort."

"What's the third thing?" Dena asked.

"I wanted to prove to you that the Bible is the truth," James answered.

"I think that one can wait for another time," Curt said politely. "This school issue and my job are the most important things right now."

"Actually, Curt," Bethany began, "I think you'll see that the two are contingent upon the one. Your family is going through a serious spiritual battle, and until you realize it, nothing is going to change."

James reached for his Bible. "Listen to this. Ephesians, Chapter Six, verse Twelve, 'For our struggle is not against flesh and blood, but against the rulers, against the powers, against the world forces of darkness, against the spiritual forces of wickedness in the heavenly places.' Curt, that's where your family is right now. And unless you have the Lord on your side, you're going to be punching at air. This passage continues: 'Therefore, take up the full armor of God, that you may be able to resist in the evil day, and having done everything to stand firm.' God tells his people that these things are going to happen, because there is a real enemy. Jesus himself said that 'The thief' or enemy 'comes to steal, kill, and destroy.' He wants to see your family go to pieces. Look what First Peter, Chapter Five, verse Eight says: 'Be of sober spirit, be on the alert. Your adversary, the devil, prowls about like a roaring lion, seeking someone to devour.'"

"Okay," Curt reacted, "so then why does God allow this? Why do bad things happen to good people?"

"Why not?" Bethany asked rhetorically. "Why do good things happen to *bad* people? Let me ask you this: When you die, what do you think happens to you?"

"I would hope we get to go to Heaven," Dena answered.

"Do you believe there is a Heaven?" Bethany asked.

"Yes, I do," Dena responded.

"I do," Curt also answered.

"So, how does one get there? What are the qualifications?" James asked.

"Well," Dena began, "you have to be good."

"Compared to whom?" James asked. "How do you judge *good*? What's the criterion?"

"Well, a lot of religions have different views about who gets to go and who doesn't," Curt answered.

"So which one do you believe? How many have you actually studied?" Bethany asked.

"Well, they all believe in God. They all say the same thing," Dena said.

"Do they?" James responded. "The Muslims say, if you don't believe Allah to be God, you should be put to death. Are you ready to become a Muslim?"

"No," Curt said quickly, "They're crazy."

"Not all of them are that way," Dena said in response. "There are a lot of good ones."

"There's that word *good* again," Bethany noted. "Yet, they all read from the same book, which tells them to do the same thing. A lot of them are not doing what their religion advocates, and yet, we think the ones that do are crazy."

Curt looked frustrated, "Okay, so who's telling the truth?"

James put on a huge grin, "That's the million dollar question, isn't it? Which means that not all roads will get you to the same place. Let's look at what the Bible says in John's Gospel, starting at Chapter Three, verse Three:

'Truly I say to you, unless one is born again, he cannot see the kingdom of God.' and verse Sixteen says, 'For God so loved the world, that He gave His only begotten Son, that whoever believes in Him should not perish, but have eternal life. For God did not send the Son into the world to judge the world; but that the world should be saved through Him.' Nothing about killing there."

"Yeah, but Jesus is the *Son* of God not God," Curt countered.

"Ah," James grinned again, "now you know what the Mormons believe. But there's got to be a way to know, right? Look what Jesus said, that no other prophet ever said. This is John Chapter Ten, verse Thirty: 'I and the Father are one.' And in Chapter Fourteen, verse Six it says, 'I am the way, and the truth, and the life; no one comes to the Father, but through me.' So there you have it. The Bible says that there is a real enemy and God sent his son to save us, and that Jesus is God, and that he is the *only* way to Heaven. Which leaves the ultimate choice for you: Either Jesus is who he says he is, or he is the greatest liar that ever lived, because those passages were written over two-thousand years ago, which means, if he's a liar, he's been deceiving people for two-thousand years; *or* he is God and the only way to Heaven. What do you say? Who do you say he is?"

The room went quiet.

"I've never heard all that before," Curt said. "I was

told that Heaven is a place where all good people go. Why is God so judgmental?"

"Because he *is* the standard," said Bethany. "And he sent his one and only son to show us what that standard is. But here's the interesting and neat thing: None of us are capable of living up to it; so Jesus, the perfect one, died for all who believe so they could be with the Father. Think of it like you being on one side of the Grand Canyon, and God being on the other side. God's side is perfect, beautiful, and peaceful; your side is corruption, chaos, and sorrow. How do you get across that huge chasm to be with God? You can't. You bring too much baggage to be with someone who is perfect and clean. But Jesus became the bridge. He was the ultimate and perfect sacrifice to allow you to be with God in Heaven. And in spite of all your baggage, he loves you so much that he took all of our punishment to give us eternal life."

Dena spoke up, "Kind of like what Kipling said, 'Greater love has no man, that he would offer his life for a friend.'"

"Actually, Kipling was quoting Jesus," Bethany corrected her. "That quote is right here in the Gospel of John."

"So what you're saying is you guys get to go to Heaven, but we don't," Curt said.

"We didn't say anything like that," James responded. "We believe the Bible is the flawless word of God, and the

Bible said that. We just read what it says. It still comes down to what you believe."

Dena's eyes began to tear up. "I don't want to be left behind. Our family needs God."

"It starts with you," Bethany told her.

"So what do I do?" Dena asked.

"You go to the Lord in prayer. You ask for forgiveness, and you invite him into your heart; and then you ask him to give you the strength and courage to live your new life and pass it on to your family," Bethany answered.

"Will you help me with this?" Dena asked.

"It would be an honor," said James.

Bethany grabbed Dena's right hand, and Dena grabbed Curt's. Curt seemed a little reluctant at first but then firmly squeezed his wife's hand. James took his other hand and Bethany's.

"Lord," James began, "we just thank you for being with us right now. Our new friends and their family need you in their lives. Lord, help them now to open up their hearts to you and allow you to radically transform them."

There was a moment of silence then Dena spoke with tears flowing from her eyes. "Lord, I need you. I'm sorry for being a lousy mom and wife. Please forgive me. I realize now that I need you. Please change my life. Thanks for bringing James and Bethany to us."

Curt was now crying. He began to pray, "Lord, I'm still just trying to figure things out. I know you're there, but I realize now that I don't know you. Lord, I've screwed-up so badly with my family. They deserve so much better than me. I just pray right now that you will forgive me and allow me to start over. Please change my life."

Now, all four of them were crying. Bethany said a last prayer. "Jesus, you have worked a miracle today. You said that once your children are yours, they can never be snatched away. Lord, give Curt and Dena the confidence that they are yours now. Help James and me to help them walk with you. Father, we know that you can make all things new. We also pray that their girls will also make a personal decision to follow you as well. In Jesus' name we pray."

And they all said amen. The four adults stood there for a moment in silence. Bethany reached over and hugged Dena. James put a hand on Curt's shoulder. They all began to smile.

Then Curt reached over to his wife, looked her in the eyes, and said, "I'm sorry. You're an awesome lady, and I'm lucky to have you. I'm going to be the leader this family needs."

"I love you," was all Dena could get through her tears. She hugged him tightly.

James broke the silence. "We'd like you to come to church with us on Sunday."

"We'll be there," Curt rapidly responded.

"There's the other two issues we need to discuss,"

James reminded them. "Your job is killing you, and that's got to stop, and we need to deal with the school."

"Well, the school is more our problem, isn't it?" Dena asked.

Bethany spoke up, "Actually, it's not. Our daughter goes there too. Besides, there are other things going on that have become a great concern to us as well."

"What else is going on; or do I want to know?" Dena asked.

"I bet a few minutes ago, it wouldn't have mattered to you, but now I think you'll be concerned," Bethany began. "The school is teaching Islam, and requiring the students to read from Islamic propaganda and dress as Muslims. The teacher is calling this a *cultural awareness* lesson."

"Are they teaching the other religions the same way?" Curt asked.

"No," Bethany answered. "And that is the other half of this issue."

"Are these the same people that preach separation of Church and State?" Curt asked again.

"Boy, he catches on fast, doesn't he?" James commented. "Bethany and I are strongly considering pulling Lisa and Chris out of the public school system. They're no longer educating kids; they're indoctrinating them."

"So what will you do, put them in private schools?" Dena asked.

"We haven't decided yet," Bethany answered. "We're leaning towards home schooling."

"Can you do that? Is it legal? What about their social development?" Dena asked.

"It's legal," James told her. "And we're betting that she'll get much better social skills outside of the school. Look at the monsters in the schools now. Besides, it's not like we're going to chain her to her bed."

"Gosh," Dena thought aloud, "Autumn would miss seeing Lisa; and now, more than ever, I want them to be together."

James put his hand to his chin in thought. "You know, after over ten years *in* the system, there's one thing I know for certain: If you want to send a message to the school system, you do it very publicly, and you hit them in their wallet."

"How do you hit them in their wallet?" Curt asked.

"ADA, Average Daily Attendance. That's how schools get their money," James explained. "It's also known as BIS, Butts In Seats. If the student is not only in school, but also in the classroom, the school loses money."

"Are you saying you want us to pull Autumn out too?" Dena asked.

"After the crap they just pulled with our daughter, I'm okay with it." Curt interjected.

"And where's she supposed to go to school?" Dena asked him.

"We put her in a private school," Curt said. "Of course, that means we get hit in *our* wallet."

"Well," James began, "hopefully when I show you my business, you won't have to worry about that."

"Actually," Bethany began to suggest, "there is another alternative: There's home schooling."

"Home schooling?" Dena asked confused. "We're supposed to be teachers?"

"That ain't gonna work," Curt added.

"What if we did it with groups of other parents?" Bethany suggested.

"What do you mean?" asked Dena.

"Here's my thinking," Bethany answered. "You're not happy with the school; we're not happy with the school. We know of other parents at our church that feel the same way. If we all teamed together, we could have something really nice—like-minded people, educating their kids the way they want to, no hidden agendas being shoved down their throats; the kids would be learning from right-minded people, who actually care about them; they would still have social interaction, and probably form closer friendships."

"Yeah, but who would teach what subjects and when and where? I'm horrible at math," Curt said.

"Right now, I'm just thinking aloud. I know people are doing it, so give me some time to make some calls, meet with some people, and do the research," Bethany explained.

"In the meantime, I think we need to send a message to the school now," James said.

"I agree," said Curt. "I want someone's butt."

James could not help to smile a bit, but he knew it was not funny to Curt. "Well, like I said, we hit them in their wallet. We may not be able to get immediate results, but we can definitely cause some well-deserved bad publicity."

"I don't want to drag my daughter through something embarrassing," said Dena concerned.

"I agree," said James.

"At the same time, I feel that we have an obligation to warn the other parents about what's going on," said Bethany. "How would you feel if we brought this before our adult church group in a low-profile way?"

"As long as it didn't hurt Autumn," said Dena.

James was still in thought. "When's the next Board meeting at the District?" he asked.

"I think it's the first Tuesday of every month, so in about two weeks," Bethany answered. "Why?"

James smiled a little. "They have an open forum time during those meetings, don't they?"

"Yeah," Bethany answered again.

"Well, those meetings are also televised to the local community, and the local newspapers are usually there too. So imagine if a large group of parents were there, and they started asking about teachers taking students for abortions behind their parents' backs, lessons that shove religions like Islam down the kids' throats, and sexual education courses that teach everyone is going to do it, and Evolution as a science. That would get the message out, don't you think?"

"I think we'd have to really plan it out carefully," said Curt. "Again, I agree with my wife; I don't want Autumn getting hurt by this."

"I think it might be a good idea to talk to her about this. It may be that she's concerned about one of her other friends going through something like this," Bethany suggested.

"Our church group meets on Wednesday night. Why don't we start there?" James suggested.

"Okay, we'll be there," Curt said.

CHAPTER 37

Kim was exhausted from another long day. Between the girls gossiping about each other, the boys fighting, and the teachers griping about every little thing, it was like reading the old *Far Side* comic with the boy raising his hand to the teacher saying, "Excuse me, Mr. Osborne, my brain is full." All she wanted to do was go home to bed. But today was the staff meeting day, and she knew it was going to be a long, heated one.

The staff slowly piled in the library. It was the only room big enough to hold the staff. For a library, it was lacking in actual books. The schools had decided that, because students were complaining more and more that they do not like to read, they would invest in books on CD. English teachers, like Mrs. Swarengen, had questioned how that was supposed to increase literacy and comprehension to no avail. As the teachers entered the room, under-the-breath comments could be heard like, "I hate these meetings"; "These things are a complete waste of my time"; and "What time does the game start tonight?"

Kim passed out the meeting agenda. The last item on the list said Hidden Agendas. Before Kim and Carl could even get started, Jo Ann Wallace yelled out, "What's this Hidden Agendas thing on the list?"

"We'll be getting to it soon enough, Jo Ann," Kim answered.

"I just don't want to be lectured to today," she shot back.

"Isn't it amazing how she always goes right for the positive?" Jeff Michael said to Wendy sarcastically.

Wendy gave a smile, "True, but I'm wondering what it's about too."

Carl covered the first four topics pretty quickly. Most of the items were minor and required very little discussion. "At this point, I'm going to turn this over to Kim. This subject is serious, and I want you to give her your full attention; that means no correcting papers, lesson planning, etc." Carl watched grade and planner books go down on the floor. "Kim is going to be talking about a touchy subject. I'm certain that it will invoke many different opinions, so I want to keep things open but positive."

"That would be a first," Jeff mumbled to Wendy.

Kim got up and walked to the center of the room.

In the back of her mind, she noted that Carl never mentioned the word "we," as in Carl and Kim.

"Good afternoon, everyone," she began. "I know we've all had a long day, and I'd love to be able to tell you that I'll keep it short, but my gut feeling tells me that it won't be." She looked around the room at the expressions on the staff's faces. Some had looks of curiosity; others looked like they were about to say, *Oh great, another long one!* "Lately, there have been some troubling issues that have come to Carl and me, and that's why *we*"— she looked over at Carl with a smile—"decided this was serious enough to bring up in this forum.

"We have been getting complaints from students and parents about teachers' opinions and views being forced upon students. We've also been hearing that if these views are opposed, the students opposing them are reprimanded for arguing and disrupting the class."

Kim was abruptly interrupted, "I think that, at this point, there needs to be official Union representation in this meeting!" Ms. Wallace shouted out.

"Here we go," Wendy said to Jeff.

"I bet we could get some good background music to go with this right about now," he said back.

"Why do you feel the need for Union representation, Jo Ann? No one is accusing you or anyone specifically of doing anything wrong. In fact, we're handling this this way so we can get the staff's input on how to solve the problem," Kim said with the most pleasant tone she could muster.

The room was quiet for a moment with all eyes on Ms. Wallace. "I can just see where this is going."

"That's very clairvoyant of you, Jo Ann," Jeff Michael said, "but right now the rest of us would like to hear what Kim has to say so we can get on with it and get out of here at a decent time."

Carl rose up out of his seat, "Hey! We're not going to do this. Let's listen and be respectful."

But Ms. Wallace would not let up. "All I'm saying is—"

Jeff had had enough and cut her off. "Nobody *cares* what you're saying!"

"Jeff!" Carl yelled out.

Jeff cooled off, "I'm sorry, Carl, but this happens every staff meeting." He turned to Ms. Wallace, "Jo Ann, you don't speak for me. If you want a Union rep, go get one; but leave me out of it." His comment brought out a couple "here heres."

Kim decided the best way to stop the commotion would be to continue her talk. "One thing I know about our staff is that we have some great teachers here, both veterans and new teachers. I think sometimes it's easy to get comfortable with how you teach the students. I know that when I was a teacher, that was an easy thing to do. The challenge with that is that every year things change. The students change, the parents change, laws change, information changes, etc. If we, as educators, don't account for that, we start to develop a my-way-or-the-highway attitude, and instead of a learning environment, we get defensive when confronted with issues that we hold sacred.

"Today's kids are way different from ten, twenty, thirty years ago. Most of them are clueless about what it means to respect authority. Today with the Internet, these kids have access to tons of information—fact and fiction. I expect that in your classrooms there will be topics that will provoke discussions and debates; and I think that's great. I think as facilitators, you *should* be asking the students questions that would challenge their thinking. It's when we start *telling* them how they should think that we start crossing the line.

"I don't know if you've noticed, but we have some sharp students this year." A few heads nodded and a couple "yeps" were heard. "Have you also noticed that we have a lot of students with strong moral values and opinions as well, both religious and non-religious? Chances are, folks, that most of them came from their parents." Kim took a drink of her bottled water.

"So what you're saying, Kim, is that they are entitled to their beliefs, but we're not?" Ms. Wallace asked in a challenging manor.

Kim kept her face as straight as possible. "What I'm saying, Jo Ann, is that these students have a right to their beliefs, and as a facilitator, they really don't need to know what yours—or anyone else's—are. I'm saying that things have changed. These students have never used a phone with a cord on it; they've never played an 8-track tape; they missed the '60's, 70's and 80's, all those decades having extremely different values being expressed. Many of you here grew up in those decades. I think it's completely appropriate for the students to know what the values were back then and what people were thinking and why, but it's not appropriate for any public school teacher to try to get students to live by them. We can't be backing kids in a corner because they don't believe what we believe. Unless a student specifically asks you one-on-one—and even then, I would use caution—your religious and political beliefs are really none of their business. The situations that are being brought to Carl and me are involving these issues. Students are telling their parents, who eventually tell us, that they are feeling intimidated in some of their teachers' classrooms."

"It sounds like you're talking about all those right-wing, Bible-thumper kids," Ms. Wallace shot out.

"Congratulations, Jo Ann," Jeff shot back, "you just made her point,"

Kim remained quiet. It was always best when someone else closed the deal for you.

"Are you accusing me of intimidating students, Jeff?" Ms. Wallace asked angrily.

"I'd call that a big yes," said Mr. Norburg, who seemed to have just woken up.

"Let's just say your opinion was heard loud and clear just now; which makes me wonder how many times the students have heard it," Jeff responded.

Carl got to his feet again. "I said that's enough!" he yelled. "We're supposed to be a team here." He turned to Kim, "I had a strong feeling this is how it would go," he said with a harsh glance.

Kim was not moved. Her face and body stayed rock-solid. "Look, folks, whether they are Bible-thumpers or tree-huggers, these students have a right to their beliefs. However, they also have *their* line. They also have to respect the views of their classmates. Students can't be allowed to just go off and offend each other either." Kim caught her breath. "Folks, our goal is not to prepare these students to pass a test; our goal is to prepare them, best we can, to be successful when they leave the classroom. If a student is expressing a strong belief that is appropriate to the lesson being taught, I think it's fine to ask them in a positive tone, 'What makes you say that?' or 'Why do you believe that?' and even follow it up with a, 'Did you know . . .' and point out another point of view, without saying, 'You're wrong!' We're educators. We're supposed to challenge their thinking. And every now and then, they can challenge ours. I know there are many kids here that know *way* more about technology than me.

"Every person in this room has his or her strengths and can learn from each other. We need to be a little more open to other people's views. We don't have to take them on as our own. Unless you hear something that sounds dangerous or potentially harmful, you should smile and deal with it.

"Are there any questions?"

Stan Norburg's hand went up, and Kim acknowledged him. "You know, a few days ago, I almost gave a failing grade to a really good student. I will tell you that I totally disagreed with the student's point of view. But the paper was extremely well written, and she defended her stance strongly. I'm thankful that I ran the situation by Kim—by accident—because I realize that my opinion would have likely shut down some really good, thought-out work. But I also see that it would have likely caused a big blow up for Kim and Carl.

"I've been teaching for twenty-three years now. I think kids are more messed-up now then they've ever been socially, but I also see that these kids are more informed today, likely due to the Internet, then ever before. I may not like it, but things have changed very quickly; and my guess is that if we don't keep up with it, we're not going to be needed much longer. Parents today know that there are other alternatives in educating their kids. If we create hostile environments in our classrooms, they will go after and find those alternatives. And my guess is that some teachers will be looking for alternative careers."

The room suddenly went quiet. Kim asked if there were any other questions or comments. Most of the teachers nodded their heads no. "Folks, one last thing:

If you are uncertain about a lesson or subject matter in your classroom, just come and ask Carl or me first. I don't want you to be feeling like you're walking on eggshells, but at the same time, be careful with subjects that can get sensitive. We really appreciate your time today. Have a great evening." And with that, the teachers began walking out. Kim could see that Ms. Wallace was still steaming from humiliation. The look on her face was one that expressed, *No one is going to tell me how to teach.* Kim would bet the farm that that is what she was thinking. And she knew that, for Jo Ann Wallace, this was not over.

CHAPTER 38

Bethany had given Pastor Jack Hobbs at Road to Calvary Church a call and told him about what had happened to her daughter's friend. She also mentioned the Islam lesson. Pastor Jack agreed that this was a huge area of concern, and he also agreed that it should be discussed at the adult Wednesday night church group. He asked if Curt and Dena might be available for a few minutes beforehand to get to know them and pray.

~

James and Curt were meeting together to discuss Curt's departure from his job. James took much time to explain the details: licensing, compensation, promotion guidelines, and other questions that Curt brought up. There was a bit of hesitation inside of Curt that James could sense.

"Is something bothering you?" James asked.

"James, the thought of not having to work my job anymore and have freedom of my time sounds wonderful, but I don't want all the money you're talking about to change me."

James smiled, "You're afraid that money will corrupt you?"

"Yeah. I don't want to turn out like one of those rich, power-hungry guys that controls people's lives."

James was laughing now. "How many really rich people have you actually met?"

"Well, I know my boss makes more than me."

"Do you think he has the same freedom I have?"

"No. He has a job like me," Curt answered.

"Let me ask you this: If you had a million dollars, would you go buy drugs with it or use it in a corrupt way?"

"Of course not!" Curt said emphatically.

"Curt, money doesn't corrupt people; it just brings out who they really are. If you're a bad person, you'll do bad things with your money; and if you're a good person, you'll do good things with your money. Bethany and I give more to church and charity now then we were ever able to before. It's so nice to know that we can do it without thinking about it. The problem is, every time you go to see a movie, the bad guy is always some rich guy who's power hungry and corrupt, beating down the little guy. Mind you, those movies are made in Hollywood, corruption central. When is the last time you saw a movie where the rich guy was generous and nice?"

Curt thought then smiled, "*Willy Wonka* when I was a kid." They both laughed. Curt told James he was ready to go forward after that.

They put together a name list of contacts and got to work setting appointments with those people. The good news was that Curt had many contacts.

"Have you spoken to your boss lately?" James asked.

"Just this morning," Curt replied. "He's not too happy with me. I told him Autumn needed my attention for a couple more days. Seriously, James, how soon do you think I can cut the cord?"

"We've just set four appointments for you, and we got your licensing process started. How many of these people on your list do you think we can bring on board your team?"

"Most of these guys are in the same boat I'm in," Curt pointed out. "They never see their families, and they're overworked. We'll get seven to ten of them."

"That will work," James told him with optimism. "I'll train you and them until you can do your own training. Just know this: For the next two to six months, you are going to be spread thin. Things will not be comfortable— balance will likely not exist. But in the long run, it will be worth it."

"Are you sure?" Curt asked.

"Oh yeah, your life will be totally unbalanced," James

said with a big smile. "Curt, are you willing to fight for your family?"

"Yep."

"Then I'll be right there to fight with you," James assured him.

CHAPTER 39

Dena went into Autumn's room to check on her. She was sitting up on her bed looking at a photo album.

"What are you looking at?" Dena asked to break the silence.

"Just some pictures from when I was a kid," she responded with little emotion

Dena moved closer to see the pictures. "I remember that day. You got pink bubblegum ice-cream all over that dress."

Autumn's eyes began to tear up. "I was a cute kid. I looked so happy here."

Dena put her arm around her daughter and brought her close. "You're still a cute kid, and you can still choose to be happy. I think we're all going to go through some changes around here. I want you to know that Dad and I are going to do whatever it takes to bring this family back together and strengthen it. I was really wrong about your dad, Autumn. He's been faithful to me. The problem is that he was becoming more faithful to his job, but that will be changing soon."

Autumn looked up at her mother, "Mom, it was awful, everything," she began, and Dena knew this was going to be painful but good for her daughter. Autumn spent about an hour telling her mom about Jorge, the sneaking out at night, the drinking, and the sexual experience she had very little memory of. Dena made a suggestion of the sexual encounter being rape. But Autumn said no; she felt just as responsible.

"I need to ask you something," Dena said. "Who took you to the clinic?"

Autumn went quiet and looked towards the floor. After about a minute, Autumn looked up at her mom. "I don't want to say," she said.

Dena tried another approach. "If I tell you who I believe it is, will you tell me?"

Autumn looked away. She was thinking about it. "Okay," she finally said.

"Was it your health teacher?"

Autumn's face looked surprised that her mom got it on the first try. She nodded up and down. "Mom, I asked her; she was trying to help me."

"Autumn, that's not the point; and it doesn't matter if she was within the law. Your dad and I are your parents."

"Dad wasn't even here," she said defensively.

"No, and neither was I. But when we both found out, we both dropped everything and came to you. Your dad left at the threat of losing his job."

Autumn looked shocked. "Did Dad get fired?"

"No," Dena answered, "but his idiot boss basically put him in a position where he had to choose his daughter over his big meeting. And your dad didn't even think twice about that. Autumn, we love our daughter. This abortion, it almost killed you. It was hard enough to get a call from your friend's mom to find out that you were in the emergency room. How do you think it would have been for us to find out you had died?" Dena asked with tears in her eyes.

Autumn was holding her mother and crying with her. It finally dawned on her how much her parents loved her. "I'm sorry, Mom."

"I'm sorry too," Dena said. She held Autumn's arms and then said, "But God had a plan in all this. God used you to get your dad and I's attention. And he got it. Your dad and I prayed to become Christians, and we prayed for our marriage and family too. We're going to live our lives differently from now on."

Autumn stayed quiet in thought. She did not know what to say or how she felt about that. "So you think God wanted me to have an abortion and then go through all the rest?"

"I don't think God wanted you to be harmed. The fact is, Autumn, we all have free-will—God didn't create puppets. We all have decisions to make, and those decisions will create consequences, good or bad. You can't blame God for *your* choices."

"Mom, I don't even know if I believe in God."

Dena felt her heart skip a beat. *What do I say,* she thought to herself. "Why not?" she asked.

"Well, it's like they teach us in science class; we evolved. And besides, you've never believed in God before."

Dena felt a jolt again. "No, that's not true. I believed there was a god; I just didn't know him. Let me ask you something: Check your heart first. Do you really believe there isn't a god? What does your heart tell you?"

"I don't know, Mom," Autumn said with doubt. "I guess I would like to believe there's someone up there who cares about us, but the world is so screwed up, how could there be?"

"Well, where do you think that feeling of there being someone up there came from? My guess is you don't feel that way when you look at apes," she said with a smile.

"I don't look at them and wonder if we're related, if that's what you mean," Autumn was smiling too.

Dena felt like she was starting to make some progress now. "That's exactly what I'm saying. Because that very thought seems utterly ridiculous, doesn't it?"

"Yeah, it does," Autumn answered.

"But does the thought of God creating you give that same feeling?"

Autumn thought for a moment, "No."

"So your doubt isn't that there is a god; you just don't know who he is." Dena let that set in on her for a moment. "Look, I'm gonna be honest with you, Autumn. I'm new to all this. I'm learning. But recently, God opened my eyes and heart. I know he is real and that he loves me. It's like a veil has been lifted from over my eyes. I suddenly feel alive. I can't even explain it. But I do know this: I want the same thing for my daughters."

Autumn looked resentful, "Mom, I don't want to be a Jesus freak like Lisa and her family."

"You mean your best friend? The one who has stood by you and prayed for you every day? The one who came to your rescue when you collapsed at her house? The one who stayed at the hospital for hours until she knew that her best friend was going to be okay? Because I'm going to tell you something, Autumn: That's the love of Jesus in her life, not some ape or ambiguous god," Dena didn't realize how much her voice had risen. "If that's what being a Jesus freak is about, then I pray we can get more of them in this world!"

Autumn had a look of surprise on her face from her mother's intensity.

"We're going to church with them tonight, and I'd like you to attend Lisa's youth class with her. I want Summer to go to the high school class too."

"Good luck with that one," Autumn said pessimistically. "Whatever, I guess I'll go. Lisa's been bugging me about going anyway."

CHAPTER 40

James, Bethany, Chris, and Lisa picked up Curt and Dena and their two daughters and headed for the church. Dena was feeling a bit nervous, but Bethany assured her that everything would go great. They met with Pastor Jack briefly before the rest of the group arrived. He was in his late forties with light brown hair. He wore shorts and a button-up short-sleeve shirt. Jack was excited about their recent decision to come to the Lord, but he was also concerned about the family.

Pastor Jack was greeting people as they came inside the room. Curt had noticed that the room was well filled with many couples. James told him that there were more people there than usual. The chairs were arranged in a circle. When everyone had taken a seat, Pastor Jack began. "Good evening everyone." They all gave a "Good evening" back. "Tonight we're going to be discussing some very important topics, so I'd like to open in prayer before we begin." They all bowed their heads. "Father, we just thank you for all you've provided for us. We pray, Lord, that you will guide us in this discussion tonight. Give us wisdom tonight. In Jesus' name we pray. Amen"

"Amen!" the group responded.

"I wanted to take a moment and read out of the Book of Proverbs. Proverbs, 22:6, says, 'Train up a child in the way he should go. Even when he is old he will not depart from it.' That's what we are called to do with our children. It's up to *us, not* our schools, daycares, or even our church. This job is on *us,* and we made the choice to bring our children into this world with God's blessing. Now we have to make sure we are teaching them right and protecting them from false teachers.

"Tonight we have some talking to do about what's being taught at our local schools. But before we do that, I'd like to welcome Curt and Dena Woods. Curt and Dena just became Christians last week, through God using James and Bethany."

Applause and "Praise God" filled the room. Curt and Dena looked a little uncomfortable.

"But God also uses trials to get our attention, and he did so with the Woods. They've been through quite a lot recently, and I promised them confidentiality in the matter. However, I can tell you that the school was directly involved in their situation, and I have had others in this group tell me about other situations that need and deserve this group's attention.

"It should not surprise us that our schools should begin to turn hostile towards the Believers. The Bible is very clear that in the last days before Christ's return that there will be false teachers, false doctrine; that right will be interpreted as wrong, and wrong will be interpreted as right. Now I cannot tell you if we are in the last days—though it *feels* like it—but I can tell you that we should be expecting what's happening. There are those who believe that we should just let it happen, as if doing nothing would bring about Christ's return more quickly. Yet, the Bible is very clear that no man knows that day. There are also those that believe that Christians should not get involved in political matters. Those people do not know how to read the Bible correctly. The Bible makes it clear that we are to be the salt and the light, and since we don't know when Christ is coming back, we need to stand up for what is right and fight the good fight—especially when it doesn't feel comfortable. You better believe that these liberals and false teachers won't let up trying to shove their doctrine down our throats. And if they can't get to us, they'll go for the next generation.

"That being said, let's talk about what's going on and what we can do about it. Here's what I've been hearing: Our kids are being forced to learn Islam, which is being taught in a very biased way, plus there is no balance with any other beliefs; they are being told that there is only safe sex, and that they are no better than animals when it comes to sex; they are being told that Evolution is a scientific fact; and when they have expressed opposition in these situations, they are treated hostile, embarrassed in front of their peers, and even disciplined for it. Did I leave out anything?"

They all looked around at each other. Finally, James spoke up, "I think you nailed it. So what do we do?"

"Maybe it would be better to first do a reality check." Jack picked up a white and purple book. "How many of you have read this book?"

Only two hands went into the air.

"This book is called *Why Wait.* It came out way back in 1987. Josh McDowell wrote it to raise awareness, especially to the Christian community, that quote Christian teens are not doing any better than non-Christian teens when it comes to abstaining from sex before marriage. Twenty-two years later, this book is even more relevant. But it's not just with sex anymore. Now Christian-raised children believe that God used Creation and Evolution together; that there was only a partial flood in a region of the world; and that the Earth is billions of years old. Here's my question to you: How many of *you* know that the Bible does not support *any* of that?" Jack paused and looked around the quiet room. "Folks, *you* are responsible for your children's foundation. If you don't have one, what do you expect them to believe? Listen to this quote: 'A Bible and newspaper in every house, a good school in every district—all studied and appreciated as they merit—are the principal support of virtue, morality, and civil liberty.' Does anybody know who said that?" There were no responses. "Benjamin Franklin, the guy that all the separation of Church and State crowd want you to believe was an atheist. The secular world knows that all it has to do is tear down the foundation, and the rest is easy. You must be solid as rocks, and I'm especially putting that responsibility on the fathers here. The Bible makes it clear that you are the head of your family, so your foundation better be in stone. There are great resources out there that teach the truth, and our church bookstore has plenty of them. When your kid comes home from school and is telling you that the science teacher just explained how the fish grew feathers and began to fly, you should immediately be picking up your Bible and say to them, 'let's see what God's word has to say about that.' Stop being lazy! The wolves are hunting your children.

"So the question was what do we do? James, you're the expert on how schools operate. What do you recommend?" Pastor Jack asked.

"I have a few ideas, some more drastic than others. It's all going to depend on how unified *we* are, and how willing they are going to be to cooperate."

"We're to the point where we're ready to pull our son out and either put him in a Christian school or home school him ourselves," Linda Holm said. "We just don't know if we can afford a private school or not; and I'm not sure if either of us are qualified to home school."

"Those were a couple of my ideas," James said. "We

can have plenty of discussion starting there." James caught his breath for a moment. "Look, I don't know how this is going to sound, so I'm just going to say it. We're dealing with big-time liberals here, and they don't like us. I got into the public school system, because I believed it needed Christians. What I learned, and what caused me to leave was that the people making policy want nothing to do with Jesus or his people. So one option we have is to go to a District meeting in a large group, and let them know how we feel about all this. That would also bring it to the attention of the other parents. And even though they may not be Christians, they probably won't like it that a lot of these issues we're talking about are being shoved down their kids' throats. Plus, the local papers will be there too. So that's one option.

"But here's the big thing I learned about the system: They really like money. If you really want to send a message, hit them in their wallets. And the best way to do that, and protect your kids at the same time, is to take away ADA money."

"What's ADA money?" one of the parents asked.

"It means Average Daily Attendance; it's the money the school gets for a child being at school," Pastor Jack answered.

"I'm no fan of the school right now," said Arlene Ramirez. "but won't that affect the other students too? And what kind of perception will the community get about us?"

"That's a valid point," Pastor Jack affirmed.

Curt suddenly decided it was his turn to speak up. "Frankly, I don't care!" he shouted out. Dena grabbed his hand. "Look, I'm not going to get into the details for the sake of my family, but they didn't give a rip about my daughter when they acted behind our backs, and it almost cost her her life. No offense to any of you, but my family comes first."

"No offense taken," said Pastor Jack. "The Bible makes it clear that we need to take care of our own families first. However, it also makes it clear that we are supposed to be the light of the world. So the question is what step do we take first?"

"I think we should present our concerns first to the District next Tuesday night," Anthony Holm suggested. "Let's see how they respond. Then we'll know just how far we need to take things."

"I think that's a good idea," a few others stated while others nodded in agreement.

"Good," said Pastor Jack. "Let's meet after church service this Sunday for a bit and discuss how we're going to present ourselves. Everyone needs to write down their concerns and suggestions—I don't want this to be a gripe session. And then everyone needs to be present at the District meeting. Let's bring this to the Lord in prayer and then we'll spend some time in fellowship."

CHAPTER 41

Jo Ann Wallace arrived at the school early. She was still livid from the meeting the day before. She went to her classroom and locked the door. She knew that her long-time friend, Ev Taver would be at the District office early. Evelyn Taver was a relic in the District. She was a thirty-three year veteran teacher and had been head of the local Teacher's Union for eight years. Ev detested school administrators and was instrumental in the resignation of the last one at her school. A true rebel-rouser, Ev made sure everyone knew who she was when she walked into staff and District meetings.

Jo Ann called Ev and explained what had happened at the staff meeting. Jo Ann even managed to muster up some tears when she explained how humiliated she felt in front of her "fellow colleagues." She also told her about the prior one-on-one meetings with Kim Faretti. "She denied me Union representation. She insisted that it wasn't a reprimand, so I wasn't entitled to representation."

"Did she document anything?" Ev asked.

"No."

"So she's a *real* girl scout," she sneered, referring to Kim. "And Mr. Lane just sat there and let it all happen, huh?"

"I think Carl was stuck between a rock and a hard place, Ev. He usually just minds his own business and stays out of ours. No, it seemed pretty clear to all of us that Faretti put him up to it. I had almost half the staff come up to me afterwards telling me that I should contact you," she lied.

"Okay, let's meet at the District office at 3:15 today to put together a strategy for Mrs. Faretti to want to take a sudden administrative leave of absence."

"That would be wonderful," Jo Ann said with a smile. "By the way, did you see that Clayton is ahead in the polls?"

"It's wonderful! And the NEA is going to be donating a lot this year to help him get elected."

"I'm tired of these Fundamentalist trying to run this country. I hope they can get some dirt on this Hopkins guy."

"Don't worry," Ev said confidently, "they'll do whatever it takes to trash him; besides, he's completely out of touch with the people. Oh, By the way, one of the speakers for Tolerance Week is a transsexual."

"That's wonderful!" . . .

CHAPTER 42

It was the first day back at school for Autumn. She was nervous. She knew how her school was: If there was some gossip out there, it would come out and be all over the school in about fifteen minutes. Curt and Dena decided to take her together; they needed to clear up the absence issue, and they wanted to have words with the administrators. Both had made phone calls to their bosses telling them they were going to be running late. Neither of their bosses was happy about it. Curt got the lecture that, "It's his job that's taking care of his family." Curt felt his stomach churn when he heard that. *What a jerk!* He thought to himself. *Never again will I allow someone else to tell me what's best for my family and when I can be with them!*

They arrived at the school and brought Autumn to the attendance office. The woman at the front desk, Mrs.

Munoz, saw Autumn and said, "Miss Woods! It's good to have you back. Where have you been?"

"She's been in the hospital," Dena said. "Here's the doctor's note."

Mrs. Munoz took the note and said, "Well, I wish you would have called. Most parents—"

Curt cut her off, "don't think about calling the school when their daughter is in the Emergency room," he said sternly.

"I'm sorry, Mr. Woods. I didn't—"

This time Dena cut her off, "We'd like to have a word with the principal. Is he available?"

"I can check," Mrs. Munoz said, as she reached for the phone. When she was done speaking to the person on the other end, she looked up at them and said, "Mr. Lane is at the District office right now for a principals' meeting, but Mrs. Faretti is here. She's out supervising the students, but she'll be in shortly after the bell rings, which will happen in about two minutes. Would you like to wait in the front office for her?"

"Sure, we'll wait," Dena said. "In the meantime, Autumn, why don't you get ready to go to your class." Autumn gave her parents a brief hug and left. Curt and Dena went out the attendance door and into the main office.

Mrs. Munoz reached for the walkie-talkie and called Mrs. Faretti. "Mrs. Faretti?"

"Yes," answered Kim.

"There are parents waiting to speak with you in the front office. I told them you'd be there after the bell rang."

"Thank you," Kim answered again.

Kim was doing morning supervision duty. This included making sure all the teachers were in the areas that they were supposed to be supervising; the students were getting off the busses in an orderly fashion; and, the one she hated the most, the food line.

The morning food line was part of the Free Lunch program, in this case breakfast. Kim hated it because it was a huge waste of food and money. The State-funded program was designed to allow families that were poverty stricken to make sure that their children would get a meal or two for the day. The legislatures believed that was the ethical thing to do. The problem was that it was a very easy program to abuse. Schools knew that the more students they had on the program, the more Federal money they would receive. In some cases, schools would just go off of a student's ethnicity and offer the program to the family whether they needed it or not and there was no accountability from the State. But that was not the worst part. The meals would come with something nutritional, like a burger, piece of chicken, an apple, or carrot. They would also come with some kind of snack like a cookie or brownie and a drink of some kind. Everyday the students would eat the snack and drink the drink, but most of the time they would leave the nutritional part of the meal. During morning breakfast or lunch time a flock of seagulls would perch on top of the buildings and wait for the bell to ring—the birds seemed to know the bells better than the students. When the bell rang, the students would leave the lunch area—without throwing their trash away—and the seagulls would take to the air, swoop down to the tables, and enjoy the "free lunch" that was conveniently left for them. *Your tax dollars at work,* Kim thought. In spite of the birds doing most of the eating, Kim still believed the program to be a joke. The joke was that most of the students on the program were overweight to obese. Kim had once heard a politician say that if they did not have the Free Lunch program, thousands of children would starve. This made Kim wonder why she never heard about children dying during spring and winter break and during the summertime.

A strange feeling crept inside of Kim, and she decided to call back to the office. "Mrs. Munoz?"

"Yes, Mrs. Faretti."

"Who are the parents?"

"Mr. and Mrs. Woods, Autumn Woods' parents."

Kim got a slight chill up her back. She had the feeling that's who it was. And, of course, Carl just happened to be off campus. "Thank you, Mrs. Munoz. Tell them I'll be right up." Kim reached at her side for her cell phone and sent a quick text message to Carl. About two minutes later, her phone vibrated. She read the text: *I understand. Do the best you can. Fill me in later.* "Gee, thanks," she said aloud. She looked up to the sky. "Any help you want to give me would be appreciated, Lord." And she made her way to the office.

A few minutes later, Kim arrived at the office. She saw a couple that looked to be in their late thirties and approached them. "Are you Autumn's parents?" she asked. She was told to never assume that just because she saw a male and female, that they were the student's actual parents.

"Yes we are," Dena answered. "I'm Dena, Autumn's mom, and this is my husband and her father, Curt." Neither Dena nor Curt offered a hand.

Kim put her hand out, "I'm Mrs. Faretti, the assistant principal. Mr. Lane, our school principal, is off campus right now in a meeting." Kim could not help to notice that her hand was still floating in the air and decided to lower it. She gestured to her office, "Would you like to come in and sit down?"

Curt said yes, and they walked into the office. "A lot friendlier-looking than my office," Curt mumbled to Dena.

Kim decided that she should break the ice quickly. "I was told that your daughter was in the hospital for a few days. I would have called you personally to ask how she was, but I felt like you might need your space."

"Do you even know who our daughter is?" Curt asked pointedly.

Kim was a bit surprised with the tone, but she was

also confident with her response. "Yes, I do. You see, as the assistant principal, I deal with more students than any other person here. Most of the time it's with disciplinary issues, but I'm outside with them every day before and after school and break and lunch, so I make it a point to get to know the kids who don't frequently make it up to my office. Your daughter is best friends with the Kaye girl."

Dena spoke up, "To be honest with you, I don't think either of us had intentions on talking with you today. We just wanted to drop Autumn off together; but since we were here, we decided to speak to the principal."

"How is your daughter?" Kim asked again.

"She is better, physically; emotionally, we're not sure yet," Dena answered.

"Who is Ms. Wallace?" Curt asked like a courtroom prosecutor.

"She's our eighth-grade health teacher." Kim left it at that for the moment. "You mentioned that emotionally, Autumn may not be okay. What do you mean by that? What happened?"

"Mrs. Faretti," Curt glared at her, "does *Ms.* Wallace make it a habit to take students to health clinics without notifying the parents, or was our daughter her first one?"

Kim felt like she was sitting in an electric chair and a jolt just went through her body. She could feel her heart speed up a bit, and her mouth went dry. "Mr. Woods," she said slowly and as non-threatening as possible, "I think it would be helpful if you could tell me what has happened, so I can understand your concern better. I don't know anything about our health teacher taking *any* student to a health clinic."

Dena became nervous. She could see the tension building quickly in her husband, and she was not ready for it. "Curt, I don't think now is the time for this. I just don't think I'm ready for it, and I don't think all the right people are here."

Curt took in his wife's words and took a deep breath. He nodded up and down at Dena. He stood up from his chair. "I think my wife is right. We'll be much more prepared to talk about this on Tuesday night. Thank you for your time."

Kim did not know what to think or say, except, "I guess I'll see you on Tuesday then." As the Woods were leaving, she called to them, "Mr. and Mrs. Woods?" They both turned to look at her. "I want you to know that I care deeply about these students. If anything unusual happens today with your daughter, I will call you personally, and don't hesitate to call me." The Woods turned and left.

Kim checked the Master Schedule to see which teachers had their prep periods now. *Oh, good,* she thought to herself, *Mr. Michael.* She went into her office and called the P.E. office.

"P.E." Jeff answered.

"Hi, Jeff, it's Kim. I need a favor from you. I need you to relieve Ms. Wallace for a few minutes."

"Sure thing, Kim."

Kim picked up her phone and called Ms. Wallace's room.

The intercom came on with a beep, "Ms. Wallace?"

"Yes."

"I need to see you for a moment. I've sent Mr. Michael to cover you class for awhile."

About five minutes later, Jo Ann Wallace arrived in Kim's office. "How can I help you?"

Kim got up from her seat and shut the door. "Have a seat," she said in a direct manner. "I just had a *very* uncomfortable—heck, I wouldn't even call it a conversation; more like a confrontation—with Autumn Woods' parents. I need a simple yes or no from you right now: Did you take their daughter to a health clinic without their knowledge?"

Jo Ann looked like she was about to rip Kim's throat open. "I will not have a conversation like this without Union representation." Jo Ann began to get up from her seat.

"Then you may want to get the Union lawyer too, 'cause these parents are ticked, and they mean business. In fact, I strongly suggest that you show up at the Board meeting Tuesday night."

"Don't tell me what to do or where to go!" Jo Ann

shot back. "I've been here way longer than you will be. In fact, your days are numbered!"

"Is that a threat?" Kim demanded.

Jo Ann flung open the door, "You're done lady!" and she walked out.

CHAPTER 43

James found himself very busy for a Monday afternoon. Curt had given him a long list of people to contact to schedule field training appointments and interviews. James was amazed at how much credibility Curt had with these people. They were all saying the same things about Curt: strong work ethic, reliable, great people skills, and they'd be happy to help him in any way. From that, James ended up booking five appointments and six interviews for Curt. "Yep," James said aloud to himself, "We'll have you out of your job really soon!"

He picked up the phone and decided to let Curt know how much success he was having.

"That's great, James! I needed some good news today."

"Is everything alright?" James asked.

"Well, we dropped off Autumn at school today, and we decided to have some words with the principal, but he wasn't there. We ended up talking with the AP, who was really nice."

"I've spoken to her before. I like her. I think she may be a Christian too."

"Well, she would have never known that I was. I was kind of a jerk—I just started reliving everything again. Anyway, I told her we would see her tomorrow at the meeting, and I think I got her guard up."

"Did you tell her why Autumn was in the hospital?"

"No, but I asked her if it was standard policy for her health teacher to take kids to health clinics without parental consent."

"Look, it's no big deal. It's all going to go down tomorrow anyway. She'll probably say something to the principal—who's kind of a wimp, by the way—and he'll alert the superintendent; but it's not going to matter. The part of the meeting we're going to go to is an open forum."

"I hope you're right," Curt said.

"It'll be okay."

"Hey, James, thanks for what you're doing for me. I want to get out of this ASAP."

"All I know is that there are a lot of people out there that like and trust you. You're going to do great at this."

"Thanks. I'll see you tonight for our appointment." Curt was tired, but knowing that he was going on his first field training appointment with James tonight gave him some extra energy.

"Sounds good."

CHAPTER 44

It was not until break time that Lisa saw Autumn. She gave her a hug and told her it was good to have her back.

"Does anyone know anything?" Autumn asked with concern.

"No. Not even Brian."

As Lisa said that, Brian came walking up and took Lisa's hand. He saw Autumn and gave her a smile. "How you feeling?" he asked.

"A lot better. I guess I owe you a thank you. Lisa told me how much you did the night I went to the hospital," she said looking at Lisa and Brian's hands together.

"I'm glad I could be there," Brian said with a smile. "I wasn't able to make it to Wednesday church, but Lisa said you were there. Did you like it?"

"Yeah, it was cool," she said still looking at the hands.

Lisa caught on to Autumn's feelings. "There were some guys there checking out the new girl."

Autumn blushed a bit. "I doubt that. Besides, I told you I only go for the older guys."

"We young guys aren't good enough for you, eh?" Brian asked jokingly.

"I think Lisa got the last good one," Autumn replied and looked down. Her eyes began to tear.

Lisa put her arm around Autumn, but before she could say anything, Brian said, "Na, we're a dime a dozen. It's girls like you and Lisa that are hard to find."

Autumn smiled. She looked up at Lisa and said, "You better not lose him."

Lisa just smiled, but Brian grinned and said, "Don't worry, she won't."

~

Just after the noon recess, Carl arrived back at the school. He walked into Kim's office. "Did you hold up the fort," he said with a smile.

"Most of it," Kim replied.

"Uh oh, which little monster attacked today?"

"It wasn't a little monster," Kim said with a serious look on her face. "It was a big one; in fact, it was Godzilla. Could you close the door?"

Carl's chipper look began to disappear. "What's going on?"

Kim told him what happened with the Woods and then afterwards with Ms. Wallace.

"Oh boy!" Carl exclaimed. "I wish you would have waited for me to come back."

"I knew you would say that."

"Kim, I don't mean that to insult you. I just . . . you know, you two aren't exactly bridge partners."

"After what I heard from the Woods, I had to know right then. And besides, Carl, I am her supervisor. She has to answer to me too," Kim explained.

"And did she admit to anything?"

"No. All she did was tell me her Union crap, and then she threatened me."

"Threatened you?" Carl responded surprised. "How so?"

"I took some time to document the conversation with quotes. This is going in her file," she handed Carl the report. "Do you know something I don't"

Carl was looking at the report. "Huh?" he looked up.

"She insisted, and I quote, 'I'm done,' and my 'days are numbered.'"

"It sounds like she wants to sick the Union on you."

"That was my thought too. Carl, I'm tired of her. She is nothing but a headache, and she's a cancer to the environment. I want her out of here."

"Good luck," Carl said with pessimism. "You and I will be gone long before her."

"It's funny you say that; that's exactly what she said— well, about me anyway," Kim paused for a moment. "Carl, is it that difficult to get rid of a teacher?"

"Yeah, it really is. Even if you try transferring a teacher to another school, they can turn it into a harassment law suite. The District get's its name dragged in the dirt in the local paper, and, of course, they don't have the money like the Teacher's Union does to go to court, so typically they have to put their tail between their legs and settle, and that's expensive too.

"So what ends up happening is the District typically moves the administrator to give the appearance that they did *something,* and the crap continues for the next guy— or gal." Carl gave Kim a serious look, "Are you sure you want to submit this?"

Kim felt that cringe in her stomach that she had been feeling more and more often. She thought for a few moments, "Is that how it is?"

"That's the system, Kim. If you want to stay in it, and eventually fill my shoes, you have to learn to work with it and the people in it."

Kim was disgusted. "This sucks! I became an administrator to make a difference, to change the image of the public school system. I wanted to show people that it can be done right; that our schools really do want what's best for the kids."

"You know," Carl began, "this may be hard for you

to believe, but at one point, even Jo Ann Wallace felt the same way you did."

"Yeah, but then it became a personal agenda."

"We all have those, Kim. Some are just nobler than others."

"Carl, this family got blind sided. Their little girl ended up at a medical clinic without their knowledge— for what reason, I don't even know."

"Oh, that's easy," Carl said confidently. "If it wasn't an emergency, and you said *clinic* and not *hospital,* it can only be one thing: She took her for an abortion."

Kim felt the electric chair again. "Abortion! Carl, it's illegal for me to give a kid an aspirin, but you're telling me she can legally take a kid for an abortion—and without the parents knowing?"

"Yep. California law," he responded a-matter-of-factly.

"I feel sick," and she really felt that way. "Carl, the Woods are planning on bringing this out at the Board meeting tomorrow night. Like it or not, the District is going to get mud in its eyes."

"I don't think they're going to publically say that their daughter had an abortion, but I will notify the superintendent. He and the Board should be ready for this."

"And what about me?"

"What do you mean?"

"You said the District won't move her, so what about me?"

"We're not even close to being there yet, Kim, so let's not push the panic button if we don't have to." Carl left her office.

I can't do this anymore, Kim thought to herself. *I can't be a part of this system.* Kim was finally starting to understand Carl as well. He was not a wimp like she thought; he was numb. The system had stripped away his heart.

Kim pulled up Autumn Woods' personal information on her computer. She saw that Mr. Woods listed a cell phone number. She was nervous, but she decided to call anyway.

"Hello, this is Curt,"

"Eh, hi, Mr. Woods, this is Mrs. Faretti from Autumn's school. Have I caught you at an okay time?" she asked timidly.

"Mrs. Faretti, I'm so glad you called," Curt said.

You are? Kim thought to herself. And she realized that he sounded pleasant as well.

"Mrs. Faretti, I want to apologize to you. I took my anger and frustration out on you, and you didn't deserve it."

Kim was really off guard now. "Thank you, Mr. Woods. Mr. Woods, I'm calling because I put two and two together, and I think I now know what's going on. If you don't want to answer my question, that's fine, because I know this is personal, but between you and me only, did your daughter get taken for an abortion by Ms. Wallace?"

Curt was silent for a long moment. "Mrs. Faretti, I feel badly about my behavior and unloading on you earlier, and you stayed so professional through the whole thing, but as far as I'm concerned, you still work for the enemy. I don't know if I can trust you. Are there other people in your office right now listening, or is this conversation being recorded?"

"Mr. Woods, you are talking to me alone right now. This conversation is between you and me, and it's not going anywhere," Kim assured him.

"Why is this information important to you?" Curt asked.

"Mr. Woods," Kim said with a deep breath, "I care about these kids. I, I pray for them every night. I don't want to see them hurt."

Curt could hear the sincerity in Kim's voice, and he decided to ask her another question. "Mrs. Faretti, are you a Christian?"

"Yes, I am," Kim answered with no hesitation.

"My wife and I just became Christians last week, and God is working on both of us. He has his work cut out for him with me. But knowing that you are a Christian, I'll go ahead and trust you and take you at your word that this is between you and me. Yes, Ms. Wallace took my fourteen-year-old daughter to a clinic without her parent's knowledge to have an abortion."

Kim could hear Curt's tone rising and anger in his voice.

"And Ms. Wallace ought to thank God that I became a Christian, because otherwise I would have torn her head off! And because our daughter is in the public school system, Ms. Wallace can't even be sued for what she did. Ms. Wallace doesn't know that my daughter had serious complications afterwards, and now, there's a strong possibility that my daughter may *never* be able to have children." Curt was breathing hard and trying to catch his breath.

Kim was silent for a moment. The phone felt like a fire was going through it. She gave him a few seconds to catch his breath before she spoke. "Mr. Woods, I'm so sorry that this happened. Had I known, I would have stopped it from happening. Thank you for telling me. This stays between you and me, and I will pray for your daughter and your family. And I will see you tomorrow night."

"Thank you, Mrs. Faretti. Until tomorrow."

And they both hung up.

CHAPTER 45

James gave Pastor Jack a late call that evening. "Hey, Jack. Are we ready to go for tomorrow?"

"I think so," Jack responded. "Do you think they know that we're coming?"

"It's a good bet. But the last hour is the open forum, and that should be plenty of time to say what we need to say. What we need to do is make sure that we get to speak first. I don't want someone starting a huge spiel about how hard it is to park at their kid's school when they come to pick them up. That alone could go forty-five minutes."

"Good point," Jack agreed. "James, I really want you in prayer about this. I know you have some pretty strong feelings and opinions about all this. I want you to allow God to use us. If things go the right way, we could really make a difference for many people and promote some positive changes."

"I'm putting on my humble hat, Jack, and I will ask God to take the lead."

~

Kim Faretti also got a late call at her home that night.

"Hi, Kim, it's Carl."

"Hi there. What's going on?"

"I wanted to let you know that I had a talk with the superintendent before I left tonight. He didn't like what I told him. He said that if these parents try to take over the meeting, he and the Board are going to shut them down."

"Shut them down? What exactly does that mean?" Kim asked.

"I think it means he's going to say, meeting adjourned, have a nice night, don't let the bed bugs bite."

"That's an open forum, Carl. He can't do that."

"Well, that's their plan. They don't want any negative situations breaking out."

"Carl, those people have the same rights as anyone else who attends a Board meeting."

"Kim, this is not our problem or our say. They're going to do what they're going to do. Don't lose any sleep over this. It's just another one of those things that we don't have control over. If the superintendent and the Board want to start World War III, let them. This is not the hill I plan to die on."

Kim was getting upset. "What hill *is* worth dying on,

Carl? That little girl was taken for an operation without her parent's knowledge by one of *our* teachers. And I know she shouldn't have been having sex in the first place, but that's not the point. A teacher played the role of parent and counselor and, as far as I'm concerned, coerced this girl into going to get an abortion. That abortion didn't agree with the girl, and she ended up in the emergency room. So I ask again, what hill is worth dying on?"

Carl was silent for a moment. "I'm sorry, Kim. I didn't realize that you took this home with you. You can't do that though. This can eat you up inside if you let it."

"Carl, all I can think is what if this was my kid. What if it was yours, Carl?"

"I understand. The good news is, it's not."

Kim was crying softly. "Carl, I don't know if I can do this anymore."

"I had a feeling you might be thinking that. I don't know how to respond either. I think you really need to give that some serious thought."

Once the conversation ended, Kim did better than that: She put her head down and prayed.

CHAPTER 46

The District office had a good size meeting room. It could seat two-hundred people at its maximum capacity. On a typical meeting night sixty to seventy people might show up. The custodian had set up his usual one-hundred chairs and left the other one-hundred stacked up in a big closet on the side of the room. As the crowd began to fill the room, it was clear to the usual attendees that the other one-hundred chairs would be needed.

Pastor Jack had persuaded the majority of the church staff to show up, a total of twelve staff members and a few spouses accompanied them. He had also called many of the church families who had attended the church for many years.

Jeff Michael was sitting next to Wendy Swarengen, and the two of them quickly noticed the larger-than-usual crowd. "Something big is brewing," Jeff commented to Wendy.

"That's for sure," she responded. "I wonder what's going on. Anything special on the agenda?"

"Not that I can see. Do you recognize these people?"

"I do recognize some of the parents. Those are Brian Holm's parents," she pointed at Anthony and Linda Holm. "Those are the Kayes."

Jeff nudged Wendy, "Take a look at the Board members' faces. They don't look too happy to see all these people."

"No, they don't," Wendy agreed. "I wonder what's going on."

"I don't know, but this ought to be good."

James walked up to Pastor Jack, "You really got the word out."

"There's strength in numbers," Jack responded.

"Looks like you brought *The 300 Spartans*."

"They're great prayer warriors, anyway," Jack said with a smile. "Are you ready?"

"I think so. There're Curt and Dena," James gestured towards the door. "Bethany and I saved them seats. I'm gonna go get them."

James walked over to greet Curt and Dena. He brought them to a row of seats where Bethany, Anthony, and Linda were sitting and talking.

Curt pulled James aside, "I have two quick things to tell you: I have three appointments for Saturday and one after church on Sunday."

"Awesome!" James exclaimed. "What's the other?"

"Mrs. Faretti called me back. We had a really good talk. I apologized for being a jerk. James, I can't get into the whole conversation right now, but I found out that she's a Christian, and I think she's on our side, as far as all the crap that's going on at the school. I could just sense that she's not happy."

"Interesting," James said. "That could be helpful in more than one way."

One of the Board members went to the microphone at the podium in the front-center of the room. "Can I have your attention, everyone?" he began. "We certainly have a packed house tonight. We have just a few items to cover at this meeting, and once we go through them, we'll be ending earlier than usual—there are a few of us that have some late obligations tonight."

James leaned backwards to Pastor Jack, "They know. They're going to try and cut us out."

"They can try," Jack responded back. "I didn't just come with church and staff members. See the dark-haired guy in the back with the glasses?" Jack motioned towards the back, corner of the room. "He's my ace in the hole."

"Who is he?"

"I'll tell you later—if I have to," Jack said with a grin.

The Board's agenda consisted of four items: special education class sizes growing, Open House night for the schools in the District, funding of art-related after school programs, and the ongoing problems with the budget.

James made a mental note that the Open Forum part of the agenda had been omitted. He told Curt in a whisper that it was the first time he had not seen that item on the agenda.

After about forty minutes of discussion on all four topics, the Board president turned to the audience. "That is the last item on our agenda tonight. You can get transcripts of the meeting on the District web site. I now move to end our Board meeting. Do I have a second?"

In lightning fast response two other members yelled out, "I second!"

And just as quick as the last response, the Board president said, "That concludes tonight's meeting. Thank you for being here." Almost on cue, all the Board members and the superintendent stood to leave.

"Just a moment," James called out, but none of them turned to look at him. "There's a group of us here that have some concerns we'd like to discuss." Still, none of the members looked up, and they were attempting to leave the room quickly. "I said there's a group of us here that have concerns we'd like to discuss with you!" James yelled loudly enough that everyone in the room—except the Board members—looked his way.

"Hey!" Anthony Holm yelled. "We have something to say to you!" But the Board members and superintendent were still heading for the exit.

Pastor Jack motioned to Mike Davies, "You and the other staff members block the doors." Mike grabbed a few of the biggest members he could find, and they formed a human wall in front of the two doors.

"Excuse me!" one of the members said forcefully. "You're in my way!" said another. But it became apparent quickly that the church staff members were not going to move.

The Board president called out to one of the District staff members, "Call for security and the police as well; tell them we have a hostile situation here!"

"I would delay that call if I were you!" another voice from the far back of the room called out. All heads turned to look at the short, dark-haired stranger wearing glasses. "I'm Tom Patrick of Patrick and Associates Law Firm. Unless you want a highly publicized lawsuit on your hands, I strongly suggest you Board members take your seats."

"We're breaking no laws here!" one of the other Board members yelled back at him. "In fact, it's your group attempting to imprison *us* against our will."

"I assure you that by not allowing people to speak at a public forum, you are violating everyone's Civil Rights, and Class Action lawsuits are *really* expensive—not to mention, there are a few more than usual newspapers in the room tonight," Tom Patrick said back.

"There's no open forum on the agenda tonight, sir," the superintendent said.

"That was very convenient of you to leave it off," Tom responded. He held up his hand with papers in it.

"I hold in my hand this Board's last three years of Board meeting agendas. The *normal* procedures of this meeting include an open forum, where concerned parents and community members can address this Board with their concerns. Your own agenda is evidence against you. I suggest that you and the other members take their seats"

The Board president stopped. He had a clear look of defeat on his face. "Motion to resume the meeting," he grumbled.

There was silence for a few seconds, and then Tom Patrick said, "Excuse me, there's no motioning here. Please continue the meeting with the normal open forum portion of the agenda."

"Very well!" the Board president coughed out. "This meeting will continue with the open forum portion. If the guard dogs at the exits can take their seats, we'll get started."

Pastor Jack shot a smile at Tom Patrick and then Mike Davies.

James came back to his seat. He looked over at Pastor Jack, "You're good!" he exclaimed in a whisper.

"No, God is," Jack said back.

James immediately put his hand up, and just to make sure that he was noticed, he stood up as well.

"Yes, sir," The Board president addressed him. "Could you please state your name for our records and what it is you would like to address this Board with?"

"Thank you!" James said politely. "James Kaye.

My daughter attends George Washington Junior High School. I'm speaking on behalf of a large group of parents and community members who are greatly concerned about some of the practices going on at the school in the classrooms. I want to make it clear that it is our desire to cooperate with the school and work together to solve the problems. We didn't come here to start a witch hunt, but at the same time, there are matters that we feel must be addressed.

"The first is that our students are being taught Islam in a very biased nature."

"Teaching about other cultures is part of the State curriculum, Mr. Kaye," one of the Board members called out.

"Excuse me, ma'am, Islam is not a culture; it's a religion, and I know that you'll want to tell me that religious history is part of the curriculum too. The problem is that there is no balance. The students are having to read a book about the Muslim culture that is extremely one-sided. And when one of the students brought in and read out of the Quran, which contradicted the book, that student was silenced and sent to the office. On top of that, the students were being required, at first, to dress up like Muslims. I have been told that that is no longer a requirement but an extra credit opportunity. We have to take issue with a few things here: One, if you're going to teach about a culture or religion, teach it right."

"What you're saying is a matter of opinion," the superintendent countered.

"Well, all I can tell you is that the young lady, whose parents are here tonight, read the actual Quran, and like it or not, it teaches that Muslims should treat non-Muslims as enemies and put them to death. We have a Quran here if you need to read it for yourself. The point is, if the students are going to be taught about a religion, let them read out of that religion's authority or don't teach it at all."

"A lot can be said about the Crusades as well, Mr. Kaye," the voice came from the side of the room. It was Mr. Norburg. "The Crusaders killed a lot of people in the name of their god."

"Yes they did, but that is a history lesson. You won't find that in a religious manuscript, and that is not a practice that goes on today."

"So you're saying Christians aren't violent?" Mr. Norburg retorted.

James did not like the distraction. "They haven't been accused of lopping off heads, blowing themselves up, and crashing planes into buildings lately. Which brings me to the second point on this issue: If you're going to teach Islam, then you need to give equal *and credible* representation to the other religions. And my third point is that an extra credit opportunity needs to be non—and I'm sorry, but I can't think of any other way to put this— offensive to others' beliefs. My daughter has no problem with doing extra credit, but not when it compromises her values. I'm guessing the Jewish, Hindu, Mormon, and Buddhist students would probably feel the same."

Kim Faretti was sitting next to Carl Lane. She looked over at Mr. Norburg with an I-told-you-so look on her face. Mr. Norburg quickly looked away.

"This guy is really something," Carl whispered to Kim.

"For the record, Mr. Norburg," James added, "I'm told by my daughter that you are a nice man, and that most of the students really like you. It's not the messenger."

"Is there anyone else with a concern they wish to talk about?" the Board president asked aloud, obviously trying to get away from James.

James was not deterred. "Excuse me. I wasn't finished. We have two other concerns we wish to bring up."

"We need to give equal time to others, Mr. Kaye," the Board president countered.

Curt stood up.

"Yes, sir?" one of the other Board members acknowledged Curt.

"Hi, I'm Curt Woods. My daughter also attends George Washington Junior High. I'd like to discuss the next item that Mr. Kaye wanted to discuss."

There were many laughs that broke out in the crowd. Even James snickered loudly.

The Board president had the look of defeat again. "Proceed, Mr. Kaye."

"Thank you. And thank *you* Mr. Woods." Again, more chuckles broke out. "Our next concern has to do with the lessons being taught in the health class."

"This is quite enough!" a woman's voice screamed out across the room. It was Ev Taver, eyes bugging out and seething red in her large, round face. "I will not stand for this *man* and *these people* having a witch hunt on our teachers."

Curt jumped to his feet. "What exactly do you mean by *THESE PEOPLE?"* he demanded.

"Let's all calm down!" the Board president called out. "Mr. Kaye has the floor now."

"I'd like to know what she means by that comment!" Curt demanded.

James motioned for Curt to calm and sit down.

"As the Union president, I want this meeting moved to a closed-door session. I will not stand for veteran teachers being publicly scrutinized!" Ev Taver yelled out again.

"This is a public, open forum," James said calmly.

"What do you know about school board meetings?" Ev asked rhetorically.

James turned and faced Ms. Taver. "Is fourteen years in the public school system, including four of those years as a school administrator, good enough for you?" James turned back to the Board. "As I was saying, we have concerns regarding the lessons being taught in the health class. Our students, while studying the reproductive system, were told that they are no better than animals, and that they *will* have sex before marriage. When a student protested that philosophy, she was publically silenced and humiliated in front of her peers. This then led to the students having to put condoms on bananas. This was all done without any parents' knowledge."

Ev Taver shouted out again. "This man wasn't in the classroom! This is all hearsay from students to their parents. He's had his turn! Let's end this now!"

"Mr. Kaye," the Board president began, "I have to agree with Ms. Taver on this. You weren't there."

"That was *my* daughter he was talking about, sir," Arlene Ramirez spoke out, "and I can assure you—based upon the phone call I received from Mrs. Faretti—that that is *exactly* what happened, as well as the condoms and bananas."

"You and your zealous group may find this hard to believe, Mr. Kaye and Mrs. Ramirez," Jo Ann Wallace called out, "but I care about these students. I'm trying to protect them from getting in compromising situations in the first place."

Her comment set James up perfectly for the final blow. "And what do you do with students that get into these *compromising* situations, Ms. Wallace?"

She hesitated for a moment, "I don't know what you're talking about."

"Isn't it true that you took a student of yours to a

medical clinic to have an abortion without her parents' knowledge?"

Murmurs broke out throughout the crowd of people, and a reporter aimed his camera at Ms. Wallace and took a picture.

"As I said, I don't know what you're talking about. And besides, the students' have a right to confidentiality, so even if I did, it's nobody else's business—especially yours!"

"So you're denying that you took a student at your school to a medical clinic for an abortion without her parents' consent?" James countered.

"That's right!" Ms. Wallace said emphatically.

Curt was rising to his feet, but before he could say a word, a woman's voice called out from the middle of the room. "She's lying!" Everyone turned to see Kim Faretti standing up with an angry expression on her face. "She most definitely did do exactly what Mr. Kaye said."

Carl Lane put his hands to his face and whispered, "It's been nice working with you. I wish you well in your next career."

Kim just gave him a cross look.

"Do you believe this?" Jeff whispered to Wendy.

"I've never seen anything like this," she responded.

"Even if she did do it," Ev Taver said defensively, "she is completely within the law. She has done nothing wrong. In fact, she probably saved the young girl from scrutiny and humiliation."

Curt was steaming, and Dena was doing everything in her power to keep him in his seat and quiet.

"Stay calm, Curt," Pastor Jack told him. "Let James handle this. He's doing great."

The room was quickly becoming chaotic, and the Board members realized they had lost control of the meeting. The Board president tapped on the top of his microphone, "We'll have order! We'll have order here! If this meeting becomes disorderly, the Board has every right to stop it." He said the last words looking straight at Tom Patrick, who gave him an affirmative nod.

The room began to calm. James was still standing. The Board president looked at him, "Mr. Kaye, the Board has heard your concerns. Thank you. You may be seated."

James did not sit. "Sir, these are not just my concerns. The parents in this room I'm representing want to know what the Board intends to do about these issues."

"Mr. Kaye, I have to agree with Ms. Taver. No laws, ed. codes, or Board policies have been broken here. It's true that some subject matter can be viewed as controversial, but when it comes down to it, that's a matter of opinion."

"Ladies and gentlemen of the Board," James addressed them, "this isn't about laws and policies and ed. codes. This is about our children and their parents entrusting you with them. We have our values too. And even though we don't expect or demand that our values be embraced by the school or the State, we would ask that they be respected and taken into consideration and not be treated with hostility."

"A school can't be everything for everybody, Mr. Kaye. Unless there are any other concerns, I move that we end this meeting at once." No one else from the crowd spoke up. "Very well, this meeting is officially over. Good night."

The Board president turned to the superintendent, and he in turn called out to Carl Lane. "Carl, could I see you for a moment." It was not a request.

Carl looked at Kim, "This is going to be about you, and it won't be good. I'll call you later tonight if you'd like."

"To let me know if I should show up tomorrow?" Kim asked.

"Yep."

"That's fine. I'll be up."

Curt looked up at James and Pastor Jack, "So that's it then? We lose?"

Pastor Jack put his hand on Curt's shoulder. "Are you kidding me! James knocked it out of the park tonight."

"But the Board isn't going to do anything," Curt insisted.

"Curt," Pastor Jack said in a comforting voice, "Every local newspaper and the local cable network saw this. They can try to hush this up, but it's going to be hard. They'll be getting phone calls for weeks. As for us, we'll just have to implement plan B."

"What's that going to be?" Curt asked.

"We'll all meet together tomorrow night and discuss the next move. But for right now, let's all go home and pray and thank God that we got our message out."

James glanced over at Mrs. Faretti. "We had unexpected help tonight, and she's going to pay the price."

They all proceeded out of the building and into the parking lot. It was dark and there were many murmurs from people talking to each other. Curt caught wind of two people talking.

"They'll fire her; you can bet on it. Her girl scout days are done," Ev Taver said.

"I did that girl a favor. I saved her years of stress and embarrassment," Jo Ann Wallace said back.

Curt let go of Dena's hand. He almost trotted over to where the two women were. "Excuse me!" he almost yelled at them. James, Bethany, and Dena all turned to look at what Curt was doing. "I couldn't help to hear what you two were talking about. My little girl almost *died* from your favor, you witch! You're lucky I didn't come down to the school and rip your head off!"

James ran over to Curt quickly.

"Are you threatening her?" Ev Taver demanded.

James grabbed Curt and pulled him in the opposite direction, "Come on, buddy."

"It's your career that's done!" Curt yelled back as James hurried him away. "Everyone knows who you *really* are now, you Nazi! I'll enjoy reading about it in the paper tomorrow morning!"

"Curt, enough, stop," James said calmly.

"I'm okay, I'm okay." Curt said back. "James, I want to say thanks to Mrs. Faretti. That's her walking over there."

Kim Faretti was walking to her car with her head down.

James and Curt regrouped with their wives and walked quickly towards Kim.

"Mrs. Faretti," Curt called

Kim turned to see the two couples coming towards her.

"I just wanted to say thank you," Curt said to her.

"You're welcome, Mr. Woods. "You put on quite a show, Mr. Kaye."

"I aim to please," James said with a smile. "Mrs. Faretti, I know how this is going to likely turn out for you."

Kim nodded up and down, "You know, I'm to the point right now where I don't really care what happens."

"I remember when James got to that point," Bethany said.

"Yes," Kim acknowledged, "I understand that you were a school administrator."

"Fourteen years in the system; four as an AP" James answered.

"What got you out?" Kim inquired.

"To be frank, crap like this. My story is a long one, and I'd love to sit down and tell it to you over lunch sometime soon."

Kim smiled, "Mr. Kaye, we're both married."

"Yes, but you would be outstanding in my business!" James complimented her.

"I'll tell you what," Kim said, "let me find out if I have a job to go back to or not first."

"Fair enough," James said. He reached into his pocket calendar and pulled out a card. "Here's my card."

Kim took the card. "Thank you."

"Oh, one more thing," Bethany said. "Tomorrow night we're all meeting at our church to discuss what we're going to do next. Would you like to come? We'd appreciate your input."

"That's possible," Kim said. "Right now, I just need to get some rest. How about I give Mr. Kaye a call if I'm coming?"

"That's fine," Bethany said.

"Thank you, again, Mrs. Faretti," Dena said.

"Goodnight, folks," Kim said with a smile.

The Kayes and Woods walked away, and Kim got into her car. Before she could start the engine, she heard a knock on her window, and Carl Lane was standing there. Kim put down her window.

"You're on paid administrative leave starting now," Carl said. "I figured I'd spare you the phone call."

"I appreciate it," Kim said with a tired voice.

"I don't think you'll be coming back."

"I don't either," Kim said. "I'll give you a call tomorrow after I'm done sleeping in."

Carl gave a half smile, "I knew you'd find a bright side. It took guts to do what you did, Kim. Probably more than I would have had. Goodnight."

"Goodnight, Carl, and thank you."

CHAPTER 47

Every now and then, James enjoyed listening to talk radio while driving in his car. This morning the radio host was talking about the story in the newspaper about "an uproar" at a local school district meeting.

Wow! James thought to himself, *We made the airwaves too.* He grabbed his hands-free device and his cell phone and called Curt to tell him what station it was on. As James and Curt were talking, callers were calling in to voice their opinions about the issues that were mentioned in the paper. "What right do schools have taking kids for abortions?" one listener asked the host. "Our schools have replaced education with politics," another protested. "Parents today are clueless. The schools have got to cover these issues," another contended. "First the government wants to tell us what we can say, then they want to tell us what we can drive, then they tax us to death, and now they want to raise our kids. Are you sure we're still in

America?" another caller countered. "We're trying to find out who this health teacher is, Ms. Wallace," the radio host said. "There's a great picture of her in the paper. She looks like a troll. We've been trying to get a spokesperson from that school district on the line with us, but no one seems to want to talk. We're going to keep talking about this and trying to get someone from the district," he said.

"I bet they don't want to talk," said Curt to James. "They got the Nazi witch's name and photo out there though; that's good. He described her well too. The school is probably getting a lot of phone calls today. Are you on your way to see those people I set up for you?"

"Yep. I told you, I'm going to build you a business, and you're going to fire your boss shortly."

"Thanks, James. Thanks for everything."

"It's all going to be good, Curt. See you tonight."

A commercial came on the radio at that moment:

A vote for Governor Clayton is a vote for change and the future.

James turned off his radio.

~

At lunch time, Lisa, Autumn, Brian, and Ken were all sitting together under a big tree.

"What do you think your parents are going to do?" Ken asked them.

"I think my parents will take me out and either home school or put me in a Christian school," Brian answered.

"Mine too," said Lisa

"I don't know," said Autumn. "They'll probably do what yours do," she motioned towards Lisa. "I just don't know if I'm ready to change schools."

"I am!" Lisa said.

"Me too!" Brian agreed.

"I guess that just leaves me to talk to the birds in this tree then," Ken added.

As they were talking, Tammy Ramirez came walking over to them and sat down. "My mom said that your dad tore it up last night, Lisa."

Lisa smiled, "He didn't really tell me about it."

"My mom said that he really let Wallace have it," Tammy added.

"Good!" Brian said.

"She didn't even look at me today," Tammy said.

"Me either," Lisa said. "I'm not upset."

"My mom said all the parents are meeting at the church tonight to decide what they're going to do. I just want out of here," Tammy said

"I want to be able to see my friends still," Autumn added.

"I don't know what they're going to decide, but I'm

pretty certain they're not going to make it so we can't see each other," Brian said, as he put his hand on Lisa's.

"I trust my parents," Lisa said. "It'll be alright."

CHAPTER 48

The room that the parents meet in at the church was even more packed out than the last time they met.

"I guess everyone read the paper this morning," Pastor Jack said to James.

"Or they were listening to the radio."

"We made the radio?" Jack asked with enthusiasm.

"Yep. I guess the local talk shows read the paper too."

"Darn!"

"What?"

"Imagine if we made it to Limbaugh or Hannity?" Jack suggested.

"I think a fist-fight would have had to broken out," James said with a smile.

"You know, my lawyer friend knows this big bouncer guy . . ." Jack said facetiously.

Curt and Dena walked in the room together late. Curt walked up to James and Jack, "I have some good news."

"What's up?" James asked.

"Summer just prayed to receive Christ."

"Outstanding!"

"That's awesome!"

"She has really enjoyed her high school group here. She said that there are a lot of kids from her school here, but she never really noticed them at school before. When she first came here on the first night, she said they really welcomed her," Curt explained.

"That's good to know," said Jack. "You never know how kids will respond to each other sometimes. I'm glad they were welcoming. Let's get this started."

Jack told the crowd to take a seat so they could get started. He led them in prayer and then began the discussion. "I'd like to get some of your responses to last night's meeting with the School Board."

Curt jumped to his feet, "I just want to say thank you to all of you for being there, and especially to James for doing such a great job of representing us."

Applause and shouts of Here, here! You were awesome! and Way to go! rang out in the room.

Arlene Ramirez stood up, "I think we're done. They basically told us to go pound sand last night, and I'm ready to pull my daughter out."

Affirmative murmurs broke out.

Another woman stood up, "I agree, but where do we pull them out to? What are our options?"

"That's a good question," Jack said. "I've done some

homework, and James sent me some information as well. But before I present the options, I want to make something clear to you. God is really working in this situation. The local papers—and the radio stations, from what I have learned—reported on last night's meeting very favorably towards us. The local community is asking questions, and they're paying attention.

"Look how many people are here tonight! Let me ask this question: How many of you here tonight *do not* attend this church? Would you please put up a hand?"

Approximately twenty hands went up.

"Look around," Jack said. "Welcome to you. I don't know if everyone here is a Christian or not, but I do know that we all want what's best for our children, and I think we saw last night that that is not the case with the school."

"That's right!" a man in the back yelled out.

James quickly stood up, "I just want to clarify that not everyone at the school or in the District feels that way. Isn't that right, Mrs. Faretti?"

Kim Faretti was almost hidden in the very back of the room. She was blushing a bit as many people turned to observe her.

"Please forgive me," Pastor Jack said. "I didn't mean to generalize like that; and thank you for being here and for what you did last night as well."

More applause broke out.

"So, back to our options," Pastor Jack continued.

"As much as I'd like to stick it to that School Board, the priority and main focus are the kids. What is best for them? One option is to get them in private schools, preferably Christian schools. Those can be very expensive, and I think some of you would have a hard time flipping the bill."

Affirmative murmurs broke out.

"Then there's homeschooling, but I know many of you are two-income families, so that could be rough too."

"We'd never be able to do it," one woman said.

"I don't know how to teach," said another.

"What about their friends? I don't want my daughter mad at me for this."

"Once again," Jack said, "we have to do what's in the best interest of the kids, even if it makes us uncomfortable or unpopular. I will tell you this: This church has decided that it is going to start a school."

"Oh, wonderful!"

"That's great!"

"It's going to take some time though, possibly a year or two, so don't get too excited," Jack warned.

Bethany stood up, "I'd like to take a shot at homeschooling. I don't know what kind of teacher I will be, but I'll learn for my son and daughter."

"We've been talking," Anthony Holm said standing, "and I think that's the direction we're going too."

A man stood up, "We just don't have that option. We need both incomes."

"Same here!"

"Us too."

"Jack," James began, "How many rooms are available during the week at the church?"

"Most of them," Jack answered.

"What if we homeschooled here together?" James suggested.

"That's an idea," Jack affirmed. "Let me throw this out to all of you. How many of you would be available once or twice a week to help out?"

Thirteen hands went in the air out of approximately sixty people.

"That's not bad," Jack commented. "Now, how many of you, who did not raise your hands, would at least look into rearranging your work schedules or seeing how flexible your bosses are for you to do so?"

Almost every hand went in the air.

"What is the daily, required minimum amount of hours for children to attend school in this State?"

"It breaks down to about four-and-a-half hours," Kim said from the back.

"Is that it?" Jack asked surprised. "What the heck are they doing with them at the school for the rest of the time?"

"Don't get us started again, Jack," Curt said sarcastically. A few laughs broke out as well.

"If we broke it down to each of you putting in an hour a week, we could do this!" Jack said enthusiastically.

"Don't we need some kind of administrator?" a man in the back asked.

"James, that's your area of expertise," Jack deferred.

"We'll likely need someone with an active credential. Jack, you may need to add another member to your staff. Can it be done?"

"Are you recruiting yourself? Jack asked with a smile.

"No, but I definitely have someone in mind," James said glancing towards the back of the room.

"You all know me; I never preach on or talk about money. I believe if the Lord wants it to happen, he'll make it happen. Though I do believe the congregation should know that we'd like to get a school up and running within the next two years. I believe we have enough concerned families here that will help find a way to make it happen, even in this economy." Jack looked towards the back of the room, "Mrs. Faretti, would you be willing to help us brainstorm some ideas in the near future?"

Kim felt like a fish out of water, but at the same time, she also felt welcomed by this crowd of people. "You can call on me."

"Awesome!" Jack responded. "I think we need to form some type of committee for this. We're going to need people to do research in many areas, talk to other families, and I think we should include as many of the kids in this as possible; let them take some ownership."

The discussion went on for twenty more minutes. A small group decided to meet again the next day to start organizing and breaking down all the areas that needed to be addressed. Bethany, Dena, Anthony, and Arlene put themselves in charge of getting things organized, and Pastor Jack said that he would recruit some of the church staff, including Pastor Mike Davies to research the legalities. Jack closed the meeting in prayer.

James immediately tracked down Kim Faretti. "Thanks for being here tonight."

"I'm glad I was here. I'd like to help you out if I can."

"That would be great. What was the result of you speaking out last night?"

"Oh, you know how schools go," Kim said nonchalantly.

"Yes, I do. They are having you take a leave of absence, aren't they?"

Kim gave a half smile, "It's paid. They have no grounds to fire me, or even make me take the leave of absence, for that matter. I figure, as long as they're going to pay me, I can use this time to think about what I want to do with my life. My husband wants me to have some down time anyway."

"Would you be interested in working with us?" James asked.

"Well, like I said, I'd be happy to help."

"No, I don't think you understand. Would you like to come and work here? Jack would like you to join the staff as the new school coordinator."

"The pastor told you that?" Kim asked with some doubt.

"No, I told him, and he agrees. He just couldn't make it official in there at the time. The point is, God is closing one door for you, but He's opening up another."

"Why aren't you jumping on it?"

"God closed that door on me a long time ago. He has me right where He wants me now. I love doing financial education. I'm really good at it."

"Really?" Kim said with a grin. "Do you rollover TSAs?"

"Is that a yes?" James asked with enthusiasm.

"Let me give it some prayer for a day or two, but I am interested."

"Sounds good, and yes, I do rollover TSAs," James said with a smile. "Can I get a contact number for you?"

She gave him her number and said goodnight. James turned and went back into the room. It was mostly cleared out now. He walked up to Pastor Jack, Bethany, Curt, and Dena.

"Did you get her?" Jack asked.

"I think we've got her. She'd like a couple days of pray time," James answered.

"We should pray for her too," Jack said. He had them

join hands, and he led them in prayer for Kim as well as the whole venture they were about to begin.

After the prayer, Jack left to go home. Curt asked James how his meetings went.

"I almost forgot to tell you. You have two new associates on your team. I'm going to field train them for you until you can do it yourself. How are you doing on getting licensed?"

"Almost finished," Curt said with a smile. "What do you think? When can I get out of my job?"

"We need to get your team wider, get you fully licensed, make sure that you can present and close without me, and most importantly, be able to field-train others. If you push yourself, I'd say three more weeks."

"Push yourself!" Dena commanded.

"I will, I will."

The two couples gathered up their children and went home.

CHAPTER 49

James and Bethany were ready for bed. It had been a long day, but Bethany was not ready to fall asleep.

"You don't look tired," James observed. "Is something on your mind?"

"Well, we've really focused on Lisa and her school, but we haven't given much thought to Chris. He's in the system too."

"Yeah, you're right," James agreed. "When you think about it, there's hardly been any drama at his school that we've heard about, but that doesn't mean it isn't happening."

"I want to talk to him about it tomorrow," Bethany said.

"Chris is in high school. Do you really think he's gonna want to be homeschooled?"

"I doubt it, but who knows. Should this be his and our choice?"

"I think so," James said. "High school is just so

different. There's so much going on, that you may not even notice things like what's going on at Lisa's school."

"His grades are great."

"Yep," James agreed. "We'll talk in the morning."

The next morning James and Bethany discussed their concerns with their son.

"It's kind of funny," Chris began, "I haven't really noticed much of that stuff at my school. Don't get me wrong, we have the partiers, and the way-too-popular crowd, but I really don't pay attention to them. And as far as the teachers go, we have some with political agendas, but I know where I stand on things—you guys taught me that—so it doesn't really bug me. Most of the people I hang around are my friends from church."

"Speaking of your friends from church, son," James began, "did you know that Lisa's best friend's sister accepted Christ?"

"Yeah, I heard about that last night. We were all happy about that."

"Maybe you can have her hang around your group at school, so she doesn't get caught back up with her old friends," Bethany suggested.

"It's funny you mentioned that, Mom, because we were planning on doing that. Besides, she's cute."

"That's my boy!" James said with a smile.

Lisa was listening to the discussion while eating her cereal. She gave a big smile.

"If you don't mind, I think I'd like to finish at my school," Chris said.

CHAPTER 50

Pastor Jack spent much of his day talking with lawyers about the home school idea. He had a handful of church staff members and some of the parents with him in the conference room on speaker phone. He did not like dealing with lawyers like most people, but the law firm he was on the phone with, he did like. The Christian Defense Council (CDC), they were one of the largest Christian law firms on the West Coast. They had started out with just three lawyers about twenty years ago, who teamed up to help a friend who was falsely being accused of sexual harassment. It had turned out that the accuser was a staunch supporter of the ACLU, and when she realized the man was a Christian, she concocted a sexual harassment accusation about him. The man was suspended from work and contacted his lawyer friends. The three young lawyers had no idea that they were going to go up against the polished lawyers of the ACLU, but when all was said and done, they were able to prove the woman's accusations were false. The woman was fired and had to pay damages, and the man returned to his job. The firm received enormous accolades from the Christian community. They sent a new message: Christians can win in court. Suddenly Christians, who before would not enter the field of Law, began to contact the firm to join. Today the firm has over twenty lawyers on its staff.

The lawyer on the phone gave Jack many suggestions on how to go about moving this venture forward within the law and how to stay compliant with the California Education Code. He told Jack and his staff to draft documents and email them to him for review, that way the loop holes could be spotted and plugged.

"In the meantime, Jack," the man began, "if your parents want to start homeschooling now, they can. All they need to do is go to the District office and fill out the paperwork. Of course, they will have to do it through the District until this all gets worked out."

"How do you think the District would respond if about thirty parents came in to move their children to homeschooling at the same time?" Jack asked.

"That's a good question. I think it would raise the Districts red flag—not that anyone is doing anything wrong. But I think they might send some intimidating people out to homes, like they did in L.A. a couple years ago, and run some scare tactics."

"Do you think we'd be better off being patient until we have our ducks in order?"

"I think it would make things easier," the man suggested.

Jack thanked the man and assigned the many areas that needed to be addressed to the group. They agreed to do conference calls a couple times a week to give updates. The goal was to have everything in place within a month or sooner, and he had one major item on his list to take care of.

Jack walked in his office and shut the door. He picked up the phone and dialed the number. "Hello, Mrs. Faretti, this is Pastor Jack. How are you?"

"Hello, Pastor Jack," Kim answered in an upbeat voice, "I am well-rested for the first time in months and actually feeling pretty good."

"I'm happy to hear that. I'm calling because we have things moving along nicely with the school project, and I was hoping that you would be joining our staff. Have you had enough time to pray?"

"I believe I have. I think God wants me to close one door and go through the open one, so I'm in."

Jack's face grew a big smile. "Well, that's an answer to our prayers too. Can we set up a time to meet? I'd like to get you going as quickly as possible. The bottom line is, I want your input ASAP."

"That sounds great," Kim responded. "Will Mr. Kaye be joining us too? I'd like to hear the opinion from another school administrator, even if he's a former administrator."

"That can be arranged. What about your current job?"

"As of right now, they're paying me while I'm sitting at home. When they make up their minds on what they want to do with me—which will likely be to *not* extend my contract—I'll let them know. In the meantime, let's move forward."

"Awesome!"

"And please call me Kim from now on."

"Thank you, Kim."

Pastor Jack and Kim set the date and time, and Jack made his call to James. James confirmed that he would be there.

CHAPTER 51

In the evening, Curt was out with James getting field trained. Curt had managed to get off work at a reasonable enough time to get out with James and learn more. Curt was spreading himself very thin. He was getting out on as many appointments as possible to learn this business quickly. He was exhausted, but he was moving forward. This was the price tag to freedom James had told him about. James had managed to hire some solid people for Curt, and they were learning and working hard. Curt had been promoted, and the money was starting to come in as well.

"As you can see," James addressed the couple, "if you stay on your current plan, you will not be able to retire until age sixty-eight, and you'll only have about $235,000 in retirement assets. How does your current plan sound to you?"

"That sucks!" the man, whose name was Larry, said disappointedly.

"What kind of retirement is that?" his wife Janet asked.

"I thought you might feel that way," James agreed. "So let me show you what we can do for you." James showed the plan that he and Curt had put together for the family. "So we'll have you out of debt, house paid off, in seventeen years, you'll be able to contribute $250.00 more to your 401(k), and by age sixty-five you'll have $646,000 in retirement assets."

"Wow! That's a big difference," Janet said.

"It still means I'm working a lot longer than I want to," Larry commented. "I wanted to be done by at least age fifty-five, so I can enjoy my retirement. But that means I won't have as much money to retire on, right?"

"You catch on fast," James said with a smile. "In order to do that, you need to make more money. Do you have a plan to do that?"

"I already hate the job I have now. You want me to get another one?"

"So, Larry, if I can show you how you can retire ten to fifteen years earlier, get out of the job you hate, and have more money in retirement, would you be interested?"

"Heck yeah!" Larry said with excitement.

"How can you do that?" Janet asked.

By the end of the night, everyone had exchanged

cell phone numbers, and Larry had four training appointments with James within the next three days.

Curt was excited as could be. *It works!* he thought to himself. *I'm going to get out of my job! Thank you, God, for putting James into my life.*

~

Jeff Michael walked into Wendy Swarengen's classroom after school.

"Have you heard anything on Kim?" he asked.

"No, everything is hush hush. Poor lady. They always seem to find a way to run out the good ones."

"I guess that means we're next," Jeff suggested.

"That would be much tougher; we're tenured," Wendy suggested.

"True. I don't know if that's a good enough reason to stay though."

"No argument there. I think Kim would have been a really good principal."

"I don't know. I think you have to be able to ride both sides of the fence, and I just don't think she could have pulled that off. She's a woman of standards and convictions, and there doesn't seem to be any room for those kinds in public education."

"I hate how true that statement is!" Wendy exclaimed. "And worst of all, it's the kids who suffer. They get taught a lack of standards by people with no standards."

"How do you stop it?" Jeff asked rhetorically.

"I don't know. The only thing that ever gets anyone's attention in public education is the almighty dollar."

"Or lack of."

"Exactly!" Wendy agreed.

CHAPTER 52

At about 8:00 p.m. the phone rang at the Kaye house.

"Lisa, phone!" Chris yelled out.

Lisa picked up the phone. "Hello?"

"Hey," Autumn's voice said in a quiet tone.

"Hey! Are you okay?"

"I've just been doing a lot of thinking about things.

"Like what?" Lisa asked.

Lisa could here Autumn begin to cry. "I want to feel better. I want to be clean. I want this emptiness to go away."

Lisa waited a few seconds, "Autumn, I only know of one way to make that happen."

"How?"

"Only the forgiveness of Jesus can take that away."

"How do you know that?" Autumn asked skeptically.

"You've been going to Wednesday night church and

Sunday school with me now for three weeks. What have you learned from people like the crippled man and Job and the woman at the well and David?"

"God forgave them," Autumn said with hesitation. "But this is different!"

Lisa gave a little laugh, "Autumn, the woman at the well had slept with many men, and David raped Bathsheba and had her husband murdered. I can assure you that if God forgave them, He *will* forgive you. I want to read one of my favorite Bible verses to you. It's in *Romans* Chapter Eight, verses thirty-eight and thirty-nine: 'For I am certain that neither death, nor life, nor angels, nor principalities, nor powers, nor things present, nor things to come, nor height, nor depth, nor any other creature, shall be able to separate us from the love of God, which is in Christ Jesus our Lord.' Autumn, you know this, but you have yet to ask God to clean and heal you. The only thing stopping you is *you*. Why don't you give him a chance to do that?"

Autumn was crying hard. "What do I need to do?"

"Let's pray together."

"Right now? On the phone?"

"Do you want to fall asleep with this unsettled and go to bed one more night feeling this way?" Lisa asked.

"No."

"Close your eyes. Let's pray together. Lord, I'm so glad that you've forgiven me every time I've messed up. And you know I've done some stupid things too. Lord, right now my best friend in the world needs you. She needs your love and grace to make her the person she wants to be. Lord, please let her know that you are here listening to her right now."

There was silence, but Lisa could hear Autumn crying. Finally Autumn spoke: "God, will you please take my pain away? I'm sorry for what I've done. Will you heal me and forgive me for being so stupid? I want to change my life now. I ask that you will come into my life and make me a new person."

Lisa was now crying as well. "Jesus, you said if we confess you, that you will forgive us. Please let Autumn know that, unlike anyone else she has ever known, you keep your promises. And Lord, I am so happy to know that I'll get to be with my best friend in Heaven. Thank you, Lord, for coming into Autumn's heart today. In Jesus name we pray. Amen."

"Amen," Autumn whispered.

"I wish you were here right now so I could hug you."

"Thanks, Lisa. You're the best friend I could ever have."

"You get to sleep in peace tonight. Autumn, tell your parents; they'll want to know."

"I will. My dad is out with your dad right now. Lisa, my dad is so excited. My parents are so thankful they met yours."

My parents think yours are great too, and my brother thinks Summer is cute."

"Really!" . . .

After the call Lisa went to share the good news with her mom.

~

James was in his home office later that evening. He was tracking his business on the computer. *Nice month*! He thought to himself. His personal cash flow was over $14,000 so far. He looked at the other agents on his team. *Awesome! They're all making money. How did Curt do?* He scrolled down to his newly-licensed reps. *Oh, man!* He picked up the phone, and Curt answered on the other end.

"Hey, buddy," James addressed him. "Lisa shared the good news with me about your daughter. That's a huge answer to prayer."

"It's been a long time since this family cried in a good way together," Curt acknowledged.

"I have another answer to prayer for you: You've got your checks coming in for this month."

"Oh, how did I do?"

"There's one for $67.00, one for $284.00, one for $661.00, and one for $1,139.00."

"Are you kidding me!"

"Nope. Congratulations! And there's more coming."

"James, if I was doing this full-time, I could double or triple that."

"My thoughts too."

"I want to do it, James!" Curt said with excitement. "I know I can do this."

"Are you saying it's time to fire your boss?"

"I think so. Let me talk to Dena and pray about this next step."

"Usually when people come to the conclusions that you just did, that's when they can go full-time."

"James, I think God wants me to go full-time now."

"I'll be right there with you, man. We'll tear it up together."

"I'll call you back in a little while," Curt told James.

"Sounds good."

A little while only took fifteen minutes. James' phone rang, and the caller ID said Curt.

"That was fast." James said.

"Dena said go for it," Curt said with excitement. "He's fired!"

James was laughing and smiling on the other end. He knew exactly how Curt was feeling—the exact same way he felt when he fired the public education system almost eight years ago. "How are you going to do it?"

"I'm burning the bridge."

"No notice?"

"Nope. He didn't give a rip about my family when my daughter was in the emergency room."

"Would you like me to film it for you?"

Curt was smiling huge. "That is seriously tempting,

but I think just having the pleasure of saying you're fired will be enough for me."

"Okay, then starting tomorrow, you need to treat your business like your job, as far as your work ethic goes. The same time you would put into your job, you need to put here, until it can run without you."

"Sounds good. I can do that," Curt agreed. "By the way, if I made a little over $2,000 and your other guys were working too—"

"How did I do?" James cut him off. "I've pulled in a little over $14,000 so far this month."

"Dang! That's awesome!" Curt took a deep breath, "Thanks, James."

"My pleasure, buddy. Go fire your boss."

~

Curt went to bed with a smile on his face. It had been a long time since he actually started dreaming big. For the first time in a long time, his life had the potential to be something special. He decided right there that he was going to win for his family.

He woke the next morning feeling nervous and excited at the same time. Dena had a smile on her face too.

"How does it feel knowing that you're about to fire your boss?" she asked.

"Can you believe I'm actually going to do this?"

"Just remember, I'm expecting within the next three months that I'm going to fire mine too."

"Absolutely! You're my partner; we're in this together."

Dena gave him a hug and a kiss, but before she could let go, Curt hugged her even tighter. "I feel like I'm falling in love with you all over again," Curt whispered.

"We haven't been like this in a long time," Dena admitted.

Just then Summer was walking by their bedroom. "Would you two like me to shut the door?" she asked with a grin.

"Nope!" Curt said with a smile. "I'm on my way to work."

"Yeah, right. Dressed like that?" Summer observed.

Curt was in shorts, a Hawaiian shirt, with a baseball cap on, and he had not shaved. "Oh, yeah, exactly like this," he answered with a big smile."

"What, are you trying to get fired?" Summer asked.

"You might say that," he said.

"Mom, is Dad okay?"

"Yes, dear," Dena said with a grin, "and he's gonna feel even better soon."

"I'll see you in a bit. When I come back, I'm going to be on the phone calling a bunch of people to set appointments," Curt said. He gave his wife a kiss and went out the door.

CHAPTER 53

Pastor Jack went to his office at the church early in the morning. He made several calls to lawyers, administrators from Christian schools, authorities from the Department of Education, and many of the families from within the church. After a few hours, he then made a call to James.

James picked up his cell, "Good morning, Jack—actually, it's headed towards afternoon. How can I help you?"

"James, God is doing a great work. I've got to tell you, this has gone very smoothly; in fact, the process is a pretty simple one. Things will be in place in a few days."

"A few days?" James asked in disbelief. "Are you sure?"

"I had the lawyers look at everything, and they said everything is in order. The Department of Education said we're good to go too. I'm gonna put a call in to Kim and tell her we're ready when she is."

"That's amazing news!"

"I'm sending a massive notice out to the church family about what they need to do, the paperwork, and curriculum."

"Jack, I'm impressed. This is great! So the kids can start next week?"

"Yep! The only rough spot is the kids will need to find some form of P.E. However, I spoke to Kim, and she says that she has someone in mind credentialed who may be willing to run a P.E. class a couple times a week for a little extra money. James, I think we may even be able to get the school up and running sooner than expected too."

"That's fantastic, Jack! Let me know how else I can help. I have put the word out to some of the more well-off people in my business about what we're trying to do. Some of them have offered donations."

"Wow! That's awesome! Alright, I'll talk to you in awhile. Check your email."

"Will do. Have a great one."

About five minutes later, James arrived at Cosmo's Limousine Service. He parked his car in the parking lot and entered the limo with a padded bag in his hand. The Limo drove off. About fifteen minutes after that the limo pulled up in front of a mid-sized office building. James reached into the bag and pulled out a small video camera. He aimed it at the front door of the building and hit the play button.

"Today is March 11th, 2009. I am filming the front

of Curt Woods' soon-to-be, former work place. Curt is currently inside firing his boss." He paused the camera and waited. James had called Dena before he left his house to find out what Curt would be wearing. He was laughing when Dena told him. The front door opened, and James saw what looked like a Jimmy Buffet fan coming out of the building. "Ah, here comes Curt now. Hey, Curt!" James yelled out the window, "You just fired your boss. What are you going to do now?"

Curt could not believe what he was seeing. He was jumping up and down with his fist in the air like Rocky on top of the steps in Philadelphia. "Oh, man! What are you doing here?"

"Get in. Is the prisoner free?" James asked.

"Oh, man! I can't begin to tell you how good I feel right now!" Curt practically yelled.

"How did it go?"

"I walked in looking like this. You had to see everyone's faces. They were doing double-takes. I could see the expressions on their faces, 'Is that Curt? What's he doing? Is he drunk?' All I could do was smile."

James was listening intently with a grin on his face.

"I walked right past his secretary, who tried to stop me from going in his office. I opened the door, and he had to have looked at me three times. His mouth dropped open, and he said, 'Curt, what the hell is this!' and I said, 'I just wanted to say goodbye.' And he said, 'Are you insane!'

and I said, 'I was when I was working for you, but I'm better now.'"

James was laughing hard. "You said that?"

"Yep! He told me I was acting irresponsibly towards my family and, that the company has treated me well. I said, 'Really? The company cares about my family?' and he said yes. And I said, 'I've worked here for eleven years and for you five. Can you tell me the name of my youngest daughter?' and he just stood there in stunned silence, and I said, 'I didn't think so.'"

"Wow!" James responded. "Then what happened?"

"I told him to send me my last check and to remember to include the vacation pay that was coming to me from not taking a vacation in three years."

The limo pulled up to an up-scale steak house.

"Ready for lunch?" James asked.

"Oh, James, I'm not dressed for a place like this."

"Not to worry," James answered. Waiting at the door were Bethany and Dena, carrying a change of clothes.

Curt turned and gave James a hug. "Thanks, James. You and Bethany have changed our lives. Thank you!"

CHAPTER 54

Kim had left two messages for two teachers to give her a call. They had both done so around noontime. The plan was, after school was out, they would meet at a Starbucks a few miles from their school.

Kim made sure that she arrived before them. About ten minutes later, Jeff Michael and Wendy Swarengen arrived. They had not seen Kim in over two weeks, and they gave her a cheerful greeting.

After some pleasantries, Kim shifted the conversation to what she wanted to talk about. "I'll be turning in my resignation tomorrow. I have a new opportunity that has a lot more promise and a lot less stress." Kim proceeded to tell them about the whole home school and private school plan. Jeff and Wendy were excited for her. "The reason why I wanted to meet with you two is because in the near future, there will be room for you. In fact, Jeff, if you would like to make some extra money, there's room for you now."

Jeff perked up, "I'm listening."

Kim told him about the part-time P.E. classes, and he told her that he was definitely interested. Both Jeff and Wendy said that they would like to be part of a Christian school.

"Kim, I'm really excited for you!" Wendy said. "Did I hear you correctly though? The kids are going to be starting soon?"

"Yes. The parents and the majority of the kids can't wait to get out. Everything is in place." She turned to Jeff, "Jeff, I'd like you to meet with me and a couple of the leaders of this group tomorrow evening. Is that possible?"

"Sure, I can do it."

"Great! Wendy, I will be in touch. If the school starts moving forward faster, I'll call you right away."

"I'm willing to help it move faster," Wendy said anxiously.

～

On Wednesday evening, the parents and children met in the church sanctuary. There were a few parent and student speakers talking about the new education venture. In all, about one-hundred, twenty-five people were in the sanctuary. Pastor Jack then opened it up to a question and answer time.

"So this is all legal and we're good to go, right?" one parent asked.

"We have the green light. As long as your paperwork is signed, you can turn it in to the county office. Mrs. Faretti is already on the books as overseer," Pastor Jack explained.

"We'll get to see our friends still, right?" a young girl asked.

"You'll be meeting here in our Sunday school rooms and the sanctuary for morning praise time. You can have break and lunch here too, as long as you keep the place clean. It is our hope that by next year, this will be your school," Jack answered.

There were a few more questions, and then Pastor Jack asked them to pray together. "Heavenly Father, thank you for blessing us with this opportunity to give our children the very best. Please put your hand on this journey we're about to embark on. Let us see your hand in all of this. In Jesus' name we pray, Amen!"

CHAPTER 55

Carl Lane was in his office. He was tired. He had been working longer hours doing the job of two administrators. His phone buzzed, "Yes?"

"Mr. Lane, the superintendent is on line three," his secretary announced.

Carl pushed the button, "Yes, sir, how are you today?"

"Carl, Kim Faretti just left here. She turned in her resignation. She did say to tell you thank you for your coaching."

"So what's next?" Carl asked.

"We'll put an ad in the *Ed-Cal* to fly an AP position. You'll have to go through résumés and do some interviewing next week. You'll probably have to work a little longer."

Any longer and I might as well just bring a change of

clothes and shower in the locker room, Carl thought to himself. "Okay, will do. Anything else?"

"That's it. Keep up the good work."

Carl put down the phone, and about two minutes later, it buzzed again. "Yes."

"Mr. Lane, it's Grace. Can I come in and show you something strange?"

Carl held back the sarcasm and told her that was fine.

A few seconds later Grace was in his office. She handed him a few sheets of paper. "Take a look at this."

"Is this today's absence list?" he said with bewilderment.

"Yes."

"Isn't the absence list usually only a page to a page-and-a-half long?"

"Exactly."

"There are four pages here. What's going on? Is there a plague or something?"

"I don't know. It's really strange though."

"Have these parents called to report?" Carl asked.

"Just the normal amount. But there's something else that's strange too."

"Oh, do tell," Carl said frustrated.

"The majority of these students are almost always in school, six of them have perfect attendance, and all of them have a 3.0 of better."

"How come the bad kids never take the day off together? Where are these kids?" Carl asked rhetorically.

"I'll start calling, but this is going to take the whole day."

"Let me know what you find out."

Carl felt another migraine coming on. He had a stack of disciplinary referrals on his desk from the last two days. There just was not enough time to get to them all.

About a half hour after Grace left his office, he began to hear a commotion in the front office. He poked his head out his office door to see what was happening. There was a long line of parents standing in front of Grace's desk. The line extended out the front door of the office.

"What's this all about?" Carl asked.

"Mr. Lane, these parents are all here to remove their children from this school. They're asking for their children's school records."

"ALL OF THEM?" Carl exclaimed.

~

The following morning inside the church sanctuary, the students were gathered together singing praise songs. Pastor Mike Davies and a couple of the students who help lead the music at Wednesday night church were leading the music this morning. Choruses of *Lord I Lift Your Name on High, Shout to the Lord,* and a contemporary version of *Amazing Grace* were being sung loudly. There was no peer pressure, no trying to look "cool" in front of your friends, and no threat of humiliation. The students were enjoying themselves.

In the back of the church Pastor Jack stood with a handful of parents. Jack had tears coming out of his eyes. He smiled and turned to James, "We have an awesome God. Look what He's done, James."

James smiled.

Curt turned to Dena, "That's our daughter singing to the Lord."

Dena hugged him as she began to cry too. "I love you, Curt. You're my man."

James Kaye put his arm around Bethany and pulled her close. "We do have an awesome God!"

ABOUT THE AUTHOR

Joe Colosimo is a former teacher and school administrator. He holds two bachelor degrees from Azusa Pacific University and a Masters in Education from CSU Fullerton. He is currently working in the financial education field helping families save money, make money, and get out of debt. He and his family reside in Chino Hills, CA.